foolish delusions

foolish delusions

a novel auto/biography

by

Anne Schuster

JACANA

First published in 2005 by Jacana Media (Pty) Ltd.
5 St Peter Road
Bellevue 2198
Johannesburg
South Africa

ISBN 1-77009-059-2

Cover design by Disturbance
Design and layout by Sarah-Anne Raynham
Printed and bound by Pinetown Printers

Photograph of author by Annabelle Wienand

See a complete list of Jacana titles at www.jacana.co.za

Acknowledgements

To the women who have participated in my writing workshops over the years, especially *The Monthlies* and *The Regular Angels* – I have learned much from you.

To the readers of the various drafts of this book – Annemarie Hendrikz, Elise van Wyk, Jane Bennett, Liz Mackenzie, Shauna Westcott, Shirley Pendlebury, Willemien de Villiers – for your care and support, and your invaluable feedback and advice throughout the process.

To Lynda Gilfillan for insightful and fearless editing.

To Sarah-Anne Raynham for exquisite book design and layout.

To Maggie Davey and Chris Cocks of Jacana, for a truly enabling process.

To Sally Swartz for advice and direction in my research around Valkenberg Asylum in the late 19th Century; and to the staff at the National Archives, National Library, UCT Library and UCT Manuscripts and Archives, for help in the research process.

To the National Arts Council for funding which enabled me to complete the book.

For all women and our 'foolish delusions'

for my great-grandmothers, Maria and Bella
my grandmothers, Eva and Anna
and my mother, Gaenor

and, as always,

for Annemarie

Stories move in circles.
They don't move in straight lines.
So it helps if you listen in circles.
There are stories inside stories
and stories between stories,
and finding your way through them
is as easy and as hard
as finding your way home.
And part of the finding is
the getting lost. And when you're lost,
you start to look around
and to listen.

—Corey Fischer, Albert Greenberg and Naomi Newman,
A Travelling Jewish Theatre, Coming from a Great Distance

Circles

circle one

ROOTPRINTS

Perhaps we are like stones; our own history
and the history of the world embedded in us,
we hold a story deep within and cannot weep
until that history is sung.

—Susan Griffin, *A Chorus of Stones*

The night outside the window waits for me to die. The air smells of rain, wet leaves and lavender, mingled with the inside smell of disinfectant – the carbolic soap they use to scrub everything here – walls, floors, linen, bedclothes, and even us. A nightbird calls over the monotone of frogs. Rain drips from the leafless vine outside. Is this my last Cape winter?

One night there will not be another day waiting at the edges of the window panes, waiting to trickle its dismal light into this ward, touching our bodies as we lie here, unrested by the long, dark hours.

The ward is strangely silent tonight. Even Dorothy, whose nights are as restless as her days, lies quietly. It is always around this time of night when sounds seem to sink into a valley of deep silence and then echo into the night. The building creaks like the restless souls in its wards. All put to bed, all working their way through the long hours, when their memories rise up through the protective coat of dreams, if they are lucky; or, like mine, through the relentless circling in their minds and the contracting in their souls as they lie awake. I have heard it said that the time between two and four in the morning, is the time when people often die. Yet I cannot manage it. Night after night I lie here, ready – and God knows, more than willing – listening for the moment when my heart stops beating. Will I recognise my last breath? Will that last heartbeat have a special sound? Could it be that one? Or this one?

When I was a child, lying small in the big dark house, in my room at the end of the long passage, I used to be afraid of dying. I wondered then, too, what kept the heartbeats and breaths relentlessly following on. Then, fearfully, I would listen for the special sound of that last heartbeat. Now, I long to die. Yet, again and again, I suck in another breath of air, and pull it into this reluctant body of mine.

Sleep does not come easily to the dying. Not when the pain from living sits in the throat, like a story wanting to be told.

We are tormented souls here, packed away from view so that we do not disturb the harmony of the ordinary lives of the world and our families. Some see that disturbance reflected in the eyes of those who creep hesitantly in on visiting days. But others, like me and Dorothy, no longer have to endure this, or the guilty relief on the faces of our families as they leave.

Only once did my children visit me here, and then only John, my eldest son, and little Georgina. John, because I think he felt responsible for my being here; and Georgina, my poor Georgina, to try to find the mother she had lost. His collar choking him, John was restrained and perfectly proper; while Georgina simply held my hand and cried. I could not even manage to squeeze hers to show that although my body is paralysed, I am still here. Surely they could hear the voice in my head telling them that I can still see and hear and feel, even if I cannot move or speak?

When they left, I knew they would not come again. Their exit had a feeling of finality. I saw in their eyes the picture of me as a pathetic woman, locked up with all these other sad women. A woman, their mother, who had killed their father.

But did I kill Trangott? Why can I not remember? I remember seeing him at the writing desk in the hotel lounge, his large body slumped sideways, the blood seeping from the wound in his throat into his white starched shirt front. And I was standing over him, a carving knife in my hand.

Could I, would I, have plunged the knife into his flesh? And am I condemned to lie here each night, unable to sleep, unable to die, until I remember? And when I do remember, who will be with me to hear my telling?

Lesson One – Rootprints

Autobiography is not the story of a life; it is the recreation or the discovery of one. In writing of experience, we discover what it was, and in the writing create the pattern we seem to have lived. Simply put, autobiography is a reckoning.

—Carolyn G Heilbrun, *The Education of a Woman*

Autobiography is the charting of a journey to discover the course a life has taken. It is the re-creation of the story of a journey, and a re-creation of oneself in the process of writing it.

We need courage to bring to consciousness stories that have lain dormant within us – sometimes for years, even centuries. We need courage to go deep into our memories and into the traces of memory, uncovering the secrets of those who have left aspects of themselves in us. We need courage to bear the sorrow of discovery.

We need courage, too, to cross the borders, the barriers, in ourselves, and in our writing. To go to the edge of the familiar places in ourselves. To do this, we need to travel light, without cleverness or artifice, or the need to impress.

The impetus to write seldom comes as an idea or a clear plan. It comes, instead, as a 'pressure around the heart'. Deena Metzger identifies this as the moment to write: 'Write. No matter what. Don't try to name it in advance, don't call it a play or poem or essay or fiction. Don't ask it to have a form or be spelled correctly, or to appear in sentences. But write...'

- *Introduce yourself.*
- *Describe a memory, a scene from your life, which tells something about who you are.*
- *Describe a private memory, one only you know about.*
- *Where do you come from? What are your 'rootprints'? Who are your ancestors? Find an ancestor whom you know little about. Start a relationship with her/him.*

Anna Bertrand,

Cape Town, 2004

My name is Anna Bertrand. I was born in Johannesburg, South Africa, on 11 December 1947, which makes me 56 years old.

I came across this workbook – *Writing the Stories of Your Life* – in the Women's Resource Centre, and decided to work through it, exercise by exercise. I have been a secret writer all my life, scribbling poems and stories when I feel strongly about things. Recently, I have felt the need to take my writing more seriously – and perhaps even to gain enough confidence to show it to someone else. Also, I want to reflect on my life – understand myself better. What are the patterns in my life? Could these provide direction for the way I live in future?

The day is warm and quiet. A Saturday afternoon in the Johannesburg suburb of Parkview in the 1950s – trees, and birds, and maids in aprons and *doeks* sitting on the trimmed, green pavements outside the houses, their time off.

I am ten. I have been out in the garden all day. Playing in my two trees. First, the tall pine tree at the back – sitting high in the branches, the sharp smell of pine gum, sticky patches on my hands and white scratch marks on my arms and legs. After lunch I climb the tree in the front garden – a spreading syringa – from which a rope-swing hangs, dangling between two gate pillars. I have been perfecting the arc of my swing from one pillar to the other. I stand on the flat top of one pillar, grip the rope, and swing through the air like an eagle swooping across a canyon. I land, my feet sure and steady on the top of the pillar opposite. Then back again, and again.

My parents' visitors arrive for afternoon tea. They have brought Gillian with them. She is a year younger than me. 'Take Gillian and go and play in the garden.' I show her the rope-swing and demonstrate the eagle swoop, then I help her climb up onto one of the gate pillars. She grips the rope, the bow in her hair white and stiff with fright. 'Push yourself off, hard,' I say. Her hands slide down the rope and she crashes face first into the opposite pillar. Screams and blood and grownups rushing down the path from the stoep, bundling Gillian into the car and hurrying to the doctor – there's a gash in her chin. Her parents are accusing. 'How could you let her do that? She's just a little girl!'

———

I am four, my brothers and I are staying with my grandparents for three months while my parents are away on an overseas holiday. The day my parents come back, we go to meet them at the airport. We get up early for the trip in the cold and dark – my grandmother, my grandfather, my eldest brother William, clever and serious with his large glasses, and my brother Charles, pushing in front to get to our parents first. When they come through the 'arrivals' door, I recognise my father, but not the woman with him, my mother.

No one else seems to notice anything strange, but I have never seen this person before. For the next few days I follow her around the house, trying to recognise her, to find the memory of her in myself. But I never do. Over time, though, she becomes less strange, and I settle into a relationship with her.

Now, after more than 50 years have passed, I look in the mirror and start to recognise her. I see her forming in the shape of my face, the way my mouth pulls down at the corners. I find my own face disappearing as hers emerges.

Perhaps we all lose our mothers at some stage, only to find them again when they begin to stare at us from the mirror.

—

I have two brothers, William and Charles Bertrand. Our father, Harry Bertrand, married our mother, May Davies, in 1939. My mother's parents were not born in South Africa – her father, David Davies, came from Wales, and her mother, Eva Green, was born in Australia. I have not been able to trace back any further as yet.

On my father's side, his father was Hermann Bertrand, born in Cape Town, and his mother was Anna Piltz, born in Austria. I could not trace her family further, but my grandfather Hermann's parents were Trangott Schultz, born in Germany, and Maria Bertrand, born in Cape Town.

—

Dear Maria

I am your great-granddaughter, Anna Bertrand.

It is the year 2004, and I am sitting here in the quiet, musty atmosphere of the South African Archives in Cape Town, trying to find out about you. You see, I'm working through a course in writing autobiography. One of the exercises in the first lesson is to find out about my ancestors.

Here, in this intimidatingly quiet place, I have before me a volume containing a copy of your death certificate.

DEATH NOTICE

Pursuant to the Provisions contained in Section 9, Ordinance 104.

Name of the deceased:	Maria Jacoba Schultz (neé Bertrand)
Birthplace of the deceased:	Cape Town
Names of the Parents of the deceased	
– Father:	John Bertrand
– Mother:	Jacoba Bertrand (neé Jansen)
Age of the deceased:	fifty-six
Condition in life (occupation):	of no occupation
Married or Unmarried, Widower or Widow:	Widow of the late Trangott Schultz, Hotelkeeper
The day of the decease:	30 June, 1894
At what house or where the person died:	Valkenberg Asylum, Cape Town.
Names of Children of deceased:	John, Hermann, Bertha, Gottlieb, Eliza, Georgina (last being a minor)
Dated at:	Cape Town
Date:	2 July, 1894
Signed by:	J H T B Schultz – Eldest son

The cold, pale light of morning begins to seep through the windows into the ward. Long shadows of the beds and cupboards appear, and then the objects themselves gradually come into being – shabby, depressing versions of their own shadows.

If I could feel my body, it would be aching. If I could speak, I too would be groaning and mumbling like Dorothy, whose silence seems to have faded like the shadows. Her words, incoherent, are about drowning – always the same – and a blue dress. I try to breathe loudly and deeply to reassure her. Are her memories as jumbled in her mind as her words? Or is she lying there, like me, watching clear pictures of her life appear behind her eyelids?

It is only now that the pictures have started appearing in my memory. For a long time, for many months, I think, after I arrived here, my mind was as numb as my body. I felt and remembered nothing. Day in, day out, I allowed the time to go by. Only now am I starting to remember, starting to allow myself to think back, only now. Perhaps it is because I am ready to die. Or perhaps I am ready to die because I am starting to remember.

This morning it is the picture of Trangott that appears, the day I met him at a Naval Ball in Simonstown. That day he had the same determined, adventurous look in his eyes as the day he decided to start the hotel. Started, incidentally, with the money my father had left us.

I noticed him immediately. He was standing to one side, his heavy muscular body looking as if it were trying to escape from his tight suit. It wasn't that the suit didn't fit him, but rather that his body's energy resented being held in by all that starch and all those buttons. All the other young men looked insipid and lifeless next to him.

My father disliked Trangott on sight. Which was possibly another reason why I was drawn to him. He was like fresh, salty sea air in a stuffy room. My soul gasped, needing to fill my lungs with his life-force. He blew like the south-easter into our lives, our quiet, dark-furnitured, airless lives, Father's and mine. Father was no match for Trangott's determination, and had no option but to step aside and allow him to marry me.

I later thought Trangott should have gone off to seek his fortune in the diamond fields – as he had originally intended when he came out from Germany – instead of marrying me and trying to hold down his restless spirit while he worked for my father. But Trangott was always torn between his need for adventure and his longing for a home and family. His mother had died when he was born, and he was brought up by his father, a General in the Prussian army, who ran the home like a military camp. Trangott seemed to find in me the soothing comfort he had never enjoyed as a child.

In an effort to subdue Trangott, Father offered him the job

of warehouse manager in his furniture business. Father's blandness and his dark house slowly turned Trangott into what seemed the perfect son-in-law. But I watched as his raw energy hardened into frustration and anger beneath the mask of the gentleman in his three-piece suit. Only I and the children ever saw the mask slip – when his temper would send us escaping to Ouma's in Constitution Street.

Ouma's house had been my refuge from the dark house all my life. Before Mother died, she and I would visit often, taking parcels of food for Ouma, who earned very little as a washerwoman, yet always had a house full of people. Oupa had been killed when he fell off the scaffolding of a building where he was working at the docks. Ouma had to bring up the children alone. She let out the front room until Mother's brother, Uncle Bennie, got married and lived there with his wife and children, my cousins. Mother and I took Ouma vegetables and meat, and even money sometimes. I don't think Father knew about it.

The day Mother died, I heard Ouma and Auntie Dinah arguing with Father about the funeral. In the end, he must have agreed to let them have the service at the Nieuwe Kerk, Ouma's church in Bree Street, and to have the tea afterwards at her house in Constitution Street.

Everyone came to tea that day. Even Father, who had not visited Ouma's house in all the years he and mother had been married. He didn't like family gatherings, he said. And certainly he was not a sociable man. Auntie Dinah said he

didn't visit because they were non-European – or Coloured –
but Ouma said, 'Shame, he's just a *snaakse* man who doesn't
like people – any people.'

The day of the funeral, he came up the road with his stiff
face, walked up the path into the house, and only stayed a
short time. Then he took me by the hand and said, 'Come,
we're going home.'

'Shame, John, let her stay,' Ouma said, 'let her stay a
while.' I thought Father was going to say no, but he looked
down and saw my face and said I could stay for a few days,
but I must be home on Sunday night because who would
make his breakfast on Monday before he went to the shop?

I kept house for Father till I married Trangott, when I
hoped we would live in a small house near Ouma, or maybe
rent her front room. Instead, we moved into the dark house
with Father.

When Father died, leaving everything to us, Trangott sold
the furniture business and turned the shop and warehouse
into a hotel. I hoped the hotel would ease Trangott's
frustration, channel his energy – and it did at first. Once
again, the south-easter blew through our lives. Only this time
it was a black south-easter, which rattled the windows and
depleted my energy.

Anna Bertrand,

Cape Town, 2004

Dear Maria

I work as a researcher – gender issues, women's rights, that sort of thing. I freelance mostly, though I am lucky to get longish contracts sometimes. Right now, I'm working on a project researching the legal rights of prostitutes – or sex-workers, as many of them prefer to be called. I spent this morning in the Cape Town Regional Court monitoring the case of a man who is accused of killing a sex-worker in Sea Point. The accused, Ralph Sebastian, is a small man with a sharp face, small popping eyes and a scraggly moustache. He has pleaded 'not guilty' to the charge of murder. Today was the bail hearing.

His lawyer, Mr Bellows, a large overweight man, didn't really bother to stand up straight while he asked for bail for his client. He leaned forward on his arms and half-raised himself from his chair.

The Magistrate asked the Prosecutor, Nikki Cody, if the State had any objections to Sebastian being granted bail.

'Yes, Your Worship, we have reason to believe that the accused has already approached and threatened a witness. He also does not have a permanent address.' Mr Bellows managed this time to heave himself to his feet, and told the court that Sebastian would be staying with his brother, a school teacher who had a house in Vredehoek.

Magistrate Van Deventer pressed his spectacles back against the bridge of his nose and held his finger there, seeming to look up into his eyebrows while he considered the matter. Then he announced that he was granting Sebastian bail of R10 000, but gave him a warning not to have contact with any witnesses in the case.

The case was postponed to next week to give Mr Bellows time to consult with Sebastian. As he walked out, Sebastian seemed pleased with himself. He looked straight at me and smiled a rather nasty smile. I'm sure he thinks he'll get away with it. Probably thinks she was only a prostitute, and who cares that she's dead. And he might be right, with this Magistrate. I've monitored cases with Van Deventer before – those post-apartheid awareness courses to help the legal profession understand their gender and race biases seem to have passed him by.

I hope Nikki stays on as State Prosecutor on his case. I know her from monitoring other rape and violence-against-women cases she has prosecuted. I've seen that behind her good-natured, cheerful appearance, she's a determined fighter for women's rights.

When I went to speak to her in the tea break, she told me the victim was a well-known sex-worker who used the name Isobel, but was identified as Pauline Fransman from Elsie's River. She was killed when she was thrown over the railings onto the rocks at Queen's Beach in Sea Point.

Her battered body was found washed up further down the beach by the National Sea Rescue, and Sebastian was arrested soon afterwards. Apparently a witness to the murder had reported the incident.

'He doesn't seem at all worried,' I said to Nikki. 'Didn't the witness identify him?'

'She did, but she's also a sex-worker – and she'd been drinking with them when it happened. His lawyer will probably try to discredit her as a witness. I'm going to have a hard job preventing him going free.' Her calm, cheerful eyes stared at me from behind her large blue-framed glasses, like a wise owl rather than the sharp hawk of a prosecutor I knew her to be.

'I know you won't let that happen. You'll find something.'

The break over, she called the next case – and I came here to Manuscripts and Archives to look for your records, Maria.

circle two

MOMENTS OF BEING

Autobiography is a collection of moments of being.

—Virginia Woolf, *Sketch of the Past*

Once again the cold morning gloom seeps over the window
sills, filling the room. There are sounds of bustle as the day-
staff arrive and walk heavily up and down corridors, banging
doors, clanging pans, clanking trolleys. Our daily wake-up
sounds. Some of us have been lying here awake for hours,
some all night. Only those, like Dorothy, who are given the
sleeping draught at night choose this time to fall into a heavy
sleep – although the draught doesn't always quieten her.

We are a strange pair to be sharing this ward. I, who
cannot speak, and she who cannot stop speaking. Even in her
sleep, her words pour out in a heap. They seem to crash into
each other in her mind, and then fall out of her mouth
jumbled and bruised, making little sense.

'Miss Feather! Dorothy!'

They always battle to wake her. Today they will not leave
her to sleep because today they have to get us all out of bed,
cleaned up, fed and seated in the day room, ready for Dr Dodds
and his guests. Once a month the Superintendent, Dr Dodds,
brings a group of guests on a tour of the Asylum – to show
them how happy and well-behaved we are.

'Miss Feather! Wake up!'

The new Head Nurse sounds determined. She lifts
Dorothy into a sitting position and wipes her face with a wet
cloth. Dorothy groans and mumbles, her eyes still closed.

'... no hands ... no feet ... can't run ... no feet ... no feet ...'

'Come on, Miss Feather, wake up please ... Here, Nurse Fraser, take her arm on that side and help me get her to the washroom. Do we have a clean gown for her?'

They'll be back for me next. Well, I won't be any trouble. Just a quick wipe-down and then heave me into the wheelchair. Maybe someone will brush my hair today. For the visit.

When I did fall asleep last night, I dreamed of my mother. Jacoba Bertrand. Jacoba Jansen, before she married my father. I remember her as a soft, round woman, until she got ill and became thin – even thinner than Father. She often used to get tired, though she never let Father see it. Ouma said it was because she worked too hard.

I heard them arguing one day when Mother and I visited Ouma. 'Jacoba, you can't do all the work yourself, the house, the cooking, and work in the shop for him. Tell him he must get a servant to help you. If he doesn't want a stranger in the house, there's your cousin Edna's girl, Lizzie, She is ready to work and they need the money.'

And so it was that Lizzie came to live in the house to help Mother with the housework and cooking while I was at school and Mother was in Father's shop.

After Mother died, Ouma and Lizzie's mother said she couldn't stay with us in the house any more, and she boarded with Mrs Mackay in Long street. Father grumbled that he had to pay her board and lodging, but Ouma said 'I'm sorry,

John, it is not proper with Jacoba gone.' Father wanted to let Lizzie go, but Ouma said, 'Maria is only nine, John, she can't manage on her own.' So Lizzie moved out and came in the mornings after I left for school to clean the house. Then she went to the shop to help Father, leaving the buying of provisions and the preparing of supper to me.

The day mother died, Lizzie woke me and said I must help her make breakfast because Mother was ill and would not be getting up. Other times Mother had been ill she never stayed in bed. She just did everything as usual and sent me to Ouma, who would make up a foul-smelling brown liquid in a jar to take back to her.

Mother was lying with her eyes closed when I tiptoed into her bedroom. Her cheeks were flushed and her forehead was wet. She had a fever, that I knew. She opened her eyes and smiled at me. 'I will be all right later,' she whispered, 'I am just tired.'

But when Father came home from the shop at lunch time, she was worse. It was a Saturday, so I wasn't at school. Father sat with her alone for a while, and then sent Lizzie to fetch Dr Hawkins.

'You stay here with her, Maria,' Father told me, 'I still have work to do at the shop.'

When Lizzie came back with the doctor, Mother said, 'Go and see Ouma, she'll have something for me.'

I put on my street boots and my coat at the front door and hurried to Ouma's, happy to get out of the house, away from that room, so musty and closed up, away from Mother's face and her strange breathing.

'Ouma, Ouma,' I called up from the street, seeing her on the little balcony.

'Maria. What is it, my child? What's the matter?'

'Mother is sick, Ouma. A fever. Dr Hawkins is there. She said to fetch something from you.'

'Come, help your Ouma put on her coat, child.'

She disappeared from the balcony. I opened the front door and went in.

Ouma was coming out of the kitchen. 'I'm going to Jacoba,' she called to Auntie Dinah. She put a jar in her basket and we left the house and hurried through the streets.

When we reached home, Dr Hawkins came out of Mother's room and spoke quietly to Ouma. I wanted to stay and hear, but I also wanted to run out the back, sit on the back doorstep, and see if the ginger cat was there.

'Your mother is very sick,' Ouma told me. 'I will stay tonight and watch her. You go and tell your father.'

When I came back with Father, Ouma was making one of her remedies in the kitchen.

'I have sent Lizzie to fetch more water from the pump. You can sit with your mother and keep her head cool with a damp cloth.' She gave me a bowl and cloth.

With clumsy hands, I moistened the cloth in the bowl of water and put it gently to Mother's forehead and cheeks. She seemed to be asleep.

When Lizzie came to sit with Mother, I helped Ouma in the kitchen.

'Your mother hasn't been well since she came to this house,' Ouma grumbled. 'It is too dark and cold. She wouldn't listen to me, though. She used to have so much life, loved singing and dancing. Before she married your father, she and her cousins went every week to the Dance Halls. Then they were still safe for young girls. Now they are full of sailors and prostitutes.' She shook her head.

Ouma sat with Mother all night. Father stayed in his study, but kept looking in on Mother. I heard him walking with his stick up and down the stairs. Lizzie groaned in her sleep, the house creaked, and the night felt heavy, and very dark.

As soon as I heard the morning sounds outside my window, I crept out of bed and went quietly through to Mother's room. Ouma was asleep in the chair at the bed, her head dropped forward on her breast, her hands in her lap. I leaned across her and touched Mother's forehead. It was cold instead of hot.

'Ouma,' I said, excited, 'Ouma, she's better.'

Ouma opened her eyes.

'Her forehead is cool, Ouma, she's better.' Ouma put her arm around me, pulling me to her breast. 'No,' she said gently, the lines on her face deeper, her eyes full of tears. 'No, my child, Ouma is so sorry. She's gone. My poor child.'

We cried then, me and Ouma, my head on her breast, her tears wetting my cheek.

Mother lay peacefully, her eyes closed, her hands folded over the quilt. I wanted to stay on Ouma's breast forever, hearing her strong heart beating, smelling her Ouma smell. I wanted everything to stop, and then to go back. To before. It had all gone too quickly. Maybe it was my fault. I was not paying attention. Perhaps I let bad things happen because I did not pay proper attention to the good things.

Ouma was in her mid-50s when Mother died. My age now. I look a little like her, but I am not as rounded. She looked like three bundles of washing – four when she had the bundle of washing on her head. Wherever you touched Ouma, or leaned against her, she was like a warm, soft pillow. Her hands, though, were wrinkled and hard from the laundry she did every day as a washerwoman. She smelled of soap and stew.

After Mother died, the house became even darker. It felt empty, and even the ginger cat seldom visited. The days were heavy and long, and I would persuade myself out of bed each day with the promise of a visit to Ouma's on my way back from school.

Father had insisted that I go to a private school – the French Academy for Young Ladies, in Roeland Street, run by Mrs Swaving. We were taught French and English, as well as Dutch, and you could take Italian, too at an extra cost. Also extra were Pianoforte, Harp, Drawing, Vocal Music and Dancing: all things Mrs Swaving and Father thought a young lady needed to marry a rich professional man and fulfil the social duties required of a wife. Ouma told me that Mother had wanted me to go to the same school as my cousins – the government Free School in Keerom Street, where most of the children from ordinary families went. But Father had wanted me to be with children whose fathers were important men in the Colony, not children of freed slaves and their descendants. 'You must learn things you will need later in life,' he said.

My cousins – the girls, that is – also learned skills suited to their station in life, things like cooking and sewing. Preparing to be servants, most probably to some of the young ladies who went to Mrs Swaving's.

I didn't really make friends with the other girls at school, but I was a good pupil, and especially enjoyed Writing and History, often winning prizes for the best results in the school. The English teacher, Miss Gunn, praised my writing ability. 'You must stay at school as long as you can, get as much education as you can,' she told me.

The one evening, just before my thirteenth birthday, Father looked up from his book and said, 'I have informed Mrs Swaving that you will not be continuing at the Academy next year. I need you to help me in the shop, and by now you have learned all you need to.'

'But Father ...' He had gone back to his book. 'Father ... I want to stay at school. I want to be a teacher.'

'That is not a job for a lady.' He dismissed my plea. You can help me in the shop until you get married and have children. Mrs Swaving agrees with me.'

That night I lay awake long after Father had passed my room on his way to bed. I lit my candle again and prayed for God to change Father's mind. I didn't want to get married and spend my days making social visits like the mothers of the girls at the Academy.

The next day I gave Father his breakfast and left without cleaning up and went to Ouma's on the way to school.

'Don't cry, my child.' Ouma soothed me. 'It is not so bad.'

'It is,' I cried. 'I want to stay at school. I don't want to work in the shop.'

'If your father has decided, there's nothing you can do. And you are a lucky girl. Most girls would love to work in a shop instead of being a servant. You are lucky to have a father who will keep you till you get married.'

So I left school at the end of the year and went to work in Father's shop every day instead. We settled into a quiet routine. Father kept to himself, and seldom went out at night. I think he often forgot I was there. After supper, I would sometimes spend evenings at Ouma's with my cousins and their friends, but would often just stay home and read. I kept house for Father and worked in the shop until I married Trangott. Then I kept house for both of them, and continued working in the shop until the children came.

Anna Bertrand,

Cape Town, 2004

Dear Maria

I had a feeling of awe when I was brought this enormous musty-smelling book, the Admission Register of Valkenberg Asylum, filled with spindly handwriting that really does look a hundred years old. How amazing to turn the pages with all these names and details of real people, and then to find yours, Maria. Maria Jacoba Schultz, admitted 29 August, 1893. Less than a year before your death. You were admitted soon after Trangott died – one month after, according to his death notice.

You suddenly seemed very real to me, as if you were breathing beside me, inside me. Perhaps these letters I write to you are like an umbilical cord, connecting me to you.

The register gives your 'disorder' as *paralysis*, and your 'form of mental disorder' as *dementia*. And here, under 'supposed cause of insanity' is written – *grief*. Dear great-grandmother, why did you die paralysed and demented with grief? Grief from what? Trangott's death?

You and the grief feel familiar, as if I've known it all my life. Thinking it was mine.

I want to know more, but your case records are missing.

'Only a few files survived from that time,' says the Manuscripts and Archives librarian. She is helpful. 'Would you like to see the file of another patient who was in the asylum at the same time?'

'Oh, yes, thanks.'

'What about this one – Dorothy Feather?'

The dusty-smelling file arrives, and I look through it. Dorothy Mary Feather, admitted two years before you, in 1891, but died in Valkenberg in 1944. She was 32 when she was admitted, and 85 when she died there, 53 years later.

Lesson Two – Moments of Being

These intense experiences of the past have an existence independent of our minds; are in fact still in existence.

—Virginia Woolf, *Sketch of the Past*

Autobiography is more than a record of events from past to present. In writing autobiography as 'moments of being', we make a vertical plunge – down into the roots of our individual being, and bring into consciousness the experiences, the moments, that have shaped us. It is about digging down, excavating through the rubble of our past, our memories, to find fragments, scraps – and in collecting these, we piece together our stories, and our lives.

In writing a 'moment', the writer must re-experience that moment. We need to put all our energy into 'being there' with what we are writing about, and no effort at all into searching for words. We pull the reader into the moment through sound, colour, smell, taste, rhythm and texture. We must not try to think of better words, but rather try to visualise, and then write what we see. If we can see it clearly, the writing is easy.

A 'moment of being' can be in the form of a scene, a vignette, a poem, poetic prose – or even a mixture of these.

- *Starting with the phrase, 'I remember', write whatever comes to mind. Allow the writing to go in whatever direction it wants to, and into any form – poetry, prose, or a mixture. Let your memories surface, and discover moments that have intensity and vividness.*
- *Choose one memory and create a scene, providing sensory detail, sound, colours, smells, tastes, textures, feelings.*
- *Start with the phrase, 'Mealtimes in our house were …', and write your memories of childhood mealtimes. End by reflecting on what you have discovered in the writing, perhaps in a letter to your chosen ancestor.*

Anna Bertrand,

Cape Town, 2004

I remember ...

I walk down the red steps onto the slasto path. Grass on either side, and trees. There is a hedge down the side of the garden. High and thick. Honeysuckle and privet. Behind me is the stoep with its comfortable chairs. Inside the house, my mother is busy with her sewing, mending, and making her famous gingerbeer; and a large black woman in maid's uniform, little cap and apron, is doing the washing, cooking and ironing.

I remember ...

A horse and cart thunders
outside the neatly trimmed
hedge of my suburban childhood –
    clippety clop clippety clop

I stand still, listening
the clippety clop is very loud
I've had this feeling before –
clippety clop
    clippety clop

A journey behind the cardboard cut-outs of my world

I am a pink little girl
in a Happy Family snapshot
I am pure white
I eat junket in the kitchen
with my nanny

I play with my nanny's daughter
in the servants' quarters
she won't colour inside the lines
of my colouring book
I give her my favourite doll

I remember ...

I go into the garden on the slasto path
to the red gate pillars
draw with a stick in the sand
under the jacaranda,
cut paths in the fur of my ugly teddy bear
with my father's hair clippers –
    clippety clop clippety clop

a horse and cart behind the hedge
        clippety clop clippety clop

I stand like a small animal
smelling danger
alert and still
trying to remember
    almost remember
something I know
    or knew
I hear my heart beating –
        clippety clop clippety clop

through the hollow caves
in my head
another memory
flying high
like a pencil-drawn swallow

there is old fear in the memory, old sadness,
forbidden places
and the sound of wings

What happens in the secret places and passages of my childhood, while the slasto path winds clearly to the red gate pillars? What happens behind the hedge, behind the sides of my eyes, in the shadows of my bedroom, beneath the trapdoor in the floorboards – that echoes the sound of a horse and cart thundering past?

—

It is just before midnight, my alarm clock gives a muffled ring under my pillow, and I turn it off before it can wake my parents. I am eight or nine. I lie there staring into the dark room, the house is quiet. My parents are asleep in their room, my brothers in theirs. I shiver under the blankets and stare up at the ceiling, glad it is too dark to see the patterns on the moulded panels that look like pale goblin faces laughing at me.

I must get up. I have to be down there at the stroke of midnight.

I search under my pillow for my torch. I turn it on and look at the clock – seven minutes to midnight.

Earlier today at school I told my friend Marguerite about the trapdoor in the floorboards of my room which leads into the cellar that runs under the whole house.

'I go down there when I want to be by myself and no one can find me.'

'Do you go at night?' She was impressed.

'Yes. In the middle of the night when everyone is asleep.'

'Aren't you scared?' Very impressed.

'Not really. I'm going down tonight – for a midnight feast.'

In my favourite books, the schoolgirls are always having midnight feasts in their 'dorms'.

I didn't tell her that I had only been down in the cellar, once, with my father, in the daytime, and that I had kept close to him while he checked for damp.

'What will you have for your feast?'

'Oh, probably condensed milk, apples and chocolate biscuits.'

I raided the pantry before going to bed, and packed a basket which waits for me, now, under my bed.

The floor is cold. I put on my slippers and dressing gown. I put my finger into the knot in the wood of the trapdoor to pull it up. It is heavy to lift, especially without making a noise, but I manage, and shine my torch into the darkness below. The dank cellar smell rises up. I take my basket by the handle, lean over the dark hole, and drop it with a dull thud onto the sandy floor below.

'Aren't there mice and rats and spiders under there?' Marguerite had asked.

'Oh yes, but I light a candle and that keeps them away.'

I hoped I was right – that my candle would be like the fire people make when camping in the wild to keep away lions and leopards.

I lower my feet onto the ground in the cellar below – cold even through my slippers – and shine my torch around. Swallow hard. No rats.

It takes my shaky fingers a few tries to light the candle and dig it into the sandy soil. I feel the cold, fine sand on my fingers. I bite into a chocolate biscuit. My mouth is dry, and bits of biscuit stick to the top of my mouth. Then I punch two holes in the can of condensed milk with my opener and suck the sweet comforting liquid into my mouth.

I hear a noise in the house above. Thud, as someone's feet hit the floor. Probably my father on his way to the toilet. I pack up my basket quickly, blow out the candle, and by the light of the torch go back to the trapdoor. I turn off the torch and wait till my father's footsteps reach my room, pause a moment, and then move on. I scramble up through the trapdoor and pull it quietly closed. I tuck my basket back under the bed and crawl, dressing gown, slippers and all, under the blankets.

I lie there, my mouth still dry, and feel tears on my cheeks. I have become a person who has a secret cellar under her room where she goes when everyone else is asleep.

—

Mealtimes in our house were predictable, regular markers in the day and week. At exactly seven o'clock every night our manservant, Happy, who doubled as a gardener by day, rang the dinner bell and we all took our usual places at the table. Dad at one end, Mom at the other, my two brothers on one side, and I opposite them. You could tell what day of the week it was by what was served at meals. The sun might change its rising and setting times with the seasons, but mealtimes in our house never changed routine.

Even just writing about it now brings a wave of restlessness over me. I feel myself withdrawing from the memories in the same way I used to want to withdraw from the table. And from the person I was. My gaze slides over the moments, trying to focus on one, but the mealtimes blur into one another.

I see the 'me' who sat at that table, meal after meal, automatically putting food on my fork, putting it into my mouth, chewing, swallowing. Sounds of knives and forks on plates, my father slurps his wine, my mother tightens her jaw. The conversation falters, fizzles out. The main course finished, knives and forks together, mouths wiped on serviettes, Mom rings the little brass bell shaped like a Dutch boy in traditional dress. Happy appears at the door in his white shirt and trousers and white gloves. He clears the plates and takes them through to the kitchen where Angelina will start washing up. Happy brings in the pudding and closes the door. We wait while Mom dishes up the canned fruit and custard. Spoons clink in the bowls. Dad slurps his custard, Mom tightens her jaw and sighs pointedly. We finish, wipe our mouths on our serviettes, roll them up, and slide them into the rings with our names on them. Mom rings the bell for Happy. I sit suspended, staring at nothing, waiting till I can excuse myself and go to my room and find myself again in my book. Always a book, a world other than my own, where I feel real.

———

Dear Maria

How is it that I feel more real in places and times where I am invisible. 'In-between' places and times – an airport terminal, on a train, in the middle of the night when everyone else is asleep, or in a place where no one knows me?

Perhaps I am always trying to escape the life that is expected of me, trying to avoid the path my life is expected to follow. At 56, I should today be comfortable, secure, and perhaps even be expecting my first grandchild. How did I escape it all? How did I become no one's wife or mother?

Actually, it was fear that saved me. Not fear of responsibility, but fear of security. The *House and Garden* variety of security. The security that is spelled out in neat houses behind walls and gates, with flower beds, trimmed hedges and mown lawns, mothers in kitchens baking, bedrooms and wardrobes and bathrooms with toothbrushes, and meals at set times. I fear the thickness of suburban air, suburban sounds, suburban thoughts, draining me of whatever makes me feel alive.

I fear being trapped around a family dinner table, the sameness of the meal, of the conversation. My claustrophobia is not of lifts or cupboards, but the suffocation of being someone's daughter, and the inevitability of going from that to being someone's wife and someone's mother. Closed into the airless cupboard of others' expectations of me.

So how did I escape this? Escape the inevitable, that mapped-out route, the blueprint of me in pretty party dresses, going out with boys (nice boys with prospects and good families); engaged to a nice, steady man with a good job; a tasteful wedding (my mother in her Mother-of-the-Bride outfit); a nice home, nice children, etc. etc. Blink your eyes and see me, blink your eyes and see my mother, blink your eyes and see her mother.

Instinctively, I knew I must step off the path.

First I stepped off into strangeness – 'She is an odd child' – and into shyness – 'She is very quiet, isn't she?' and 'Why don't you go and play with the other children?'

Then, into eccentricity – 'Why can't you be like other teenage girls? It's not normal to sit up trees at your age or play soccer with boys, or listen to opera at two in the morning.'

And finally, I stepped off into, oh what good fortune, into falling in love. With a girl.

'I hope it's just a phase,' they said.

It wasn't.

I was surprised to see Dorothy here, in Valkenberg Asylum.
Her father, Dr James Feather, had been a regular visitor to our
hotel lounge at night. I always thought he merely pretended
to be a friend of Trangott's so he didn't have to pay for his
whisky and cigars like the other hotel guests. And Trangott
allowed him this – even liking him, I think.

They were strangely alike, though James Feather was as
small and wiry as Trangott was large and fleshy. James Feather
would make directly for the red leather armchair each night
when he arrived. I suspect because it was high and made him
feel taller. I could never understand why Trangott put up with
him and listened to his stories. When they were together they
reminded me of two teenage boys – trying to impress each
other with their boasting.

James Feather had two daughters, Dorothy and Hester.
They were delicate, like their mother, who died soon after they
all came out from England. The two girls kept house for their
father after their mother's death. In the beginning I would see
Dorothy at Mr Gruneberg's confectionery in Long Street or at
Stigling's, the butcher. She was quiet then, and anxious-
looking, like a scared rabbit expecting a fox at every corner.

Later we heard that Dorothy and Hester had gone back to
England. And now I find Dorothy here – still staring and
anxious, but no longer quiet. She cannot keep still, and tries

continually to tell people some sort of story. I'm not sure if she remembers me, although she always comes to sit close to me in the day room, and whispers her incoherent phrases. It doesn't seem to matter to her that I cannot speak – in fact I think it comforts and calms her.

'Good morning, ladies!' Dr Dodds appears at the door of the day room. Such a rooster of a man, ruffles and lace up to his ears, his chest out, strutting about. He looks around at us and seems disappointed to find how shabby we, his old hens, are.

'And here we have the European Female inmates,' he announces in his high-pitched voice to the prim-looking group, huddled together and blinking through their spectacles.

Nurse Fraser has managed to get Dorothy settled before the tour begins. She is sitting in the chair next to my wheelchair, looking a lot like her mother did, thin and bent, and with a hollow look around her eyes, caves of fear she cannot escape from. Dorothy has her needlework on her lap, but she doesn't seem to be sewing. Just sticking the needle in and pulling it out. No thread.

She's whimpering and muttering. It is as if something upsetting comes into her mind and she has to chatter it out, talking in fast, broken sentences, at times repeating the same phrase over and over. Sometimes there is a laugh, as if she is brushing crumbs from her mind – brushing them away with a hard, short laugh.

'This is the day room where those patients who are not employed in the kitchen or laundry, are engaged in useful needlework,' Dr Dodds explains.

'All paying patients, of course!' he assures them. 'A better class of lunatic. Just what this Asylum was built for. There was nothing suitable until now. Just Robben Island, with its lepers and criminals, and the Somerset Hospital, where there are people in chains sleeping on floors, amid vermin and disease – fit only for natives and Hottentots.'

Two ladies from his party have stopped in front of Dorothy to admire her handiwork. Suddenly they propel themselves backwards as Dorothy gives a shrill scream and starts pawing at them, saying over and over: '... water ... drowning ... blood ... can't run ... no feet ... water ... blood ... water ...'

'Nurse!' Dr Dodds calls down the corridor. 'Nurse! Miss Feather requires attention.' He shepherds the group towards the door. 'Let us inspect the kitchens.'

'Unfortunate woman.' He soothes them. 'A hereditary weakness, you know. She suffers from Foolish Delusions. We have to sedate her from time to time.'

Dorothy often embarrasses Dr Dodds. I suspect she plays up to him. I wonder if it's because he is like her father. Both strutting men who think they control the world. James Feather annoyed me, night after night at the Germania. He would sneer about his daughters, and about the fact that their mother was from an upper-class British family. He, himself, came from poor working-class stock, and was proud of the fact that he had been a bright lad, and had managed to move himself up in the world by studying medicine. But even though he was a doctor, her parents had not welcomed him into the family. He told us they considered him a common upstart from the slums of London, and were pleased to see the last of him when he was offered a post at the newly-built Lock Hospital in Cape Town.

I remember the first time I saw Dorothy and her mother, soon after they arrived in Cape Town. Dorothy, a pale, thin young woman, and her mother looking like a sickly crane. I welcomed them to Cape Town and said I hoped they had settled in comfortably. 'Perhaps you would like to come for tea one afternoon,' I offered.

Mrs Feather looked around, as if afraid of being overheard, 'Oh, thank you, but we don't go out much. My husband doesn't approve.' She took hold of Dorothy's arm and hurried away.

'All that breeding,' James Feather said one night, well into Trangott's whisky, 'makes them weak and pathetic. Give me a mongrel bitch any day!'

After her mother died, Dorothy grew even more anxious. Most of the time she would not look at anyone and seemed afraid to be looked at or touched. At other times, she would attach herself to someone and jabber away compulsively and incomprehensibly.

'Bad blood,' Feather told Trangott and me another night. 'Her mother was also deranged! I have stopped her going out and bothering people.' Later, he told us he had sent the two girls to their grandparents in England. 'I haven't time to bother with hysterical females.'

He used to boast about Dr Dodds being his friend, having known him from medical school in London. So, when I found Dorothy here, I assumed he had arranged with Dr Dodds to have the girls admitted. I haven't seen Hester, though. Perhaps she did go to her grandparents after all.

circle three

THE PRESENCE OF THE PAST

*No detail that enters the mind, nor the smallest instance
of memory, ever really leaves it, and things we had
thought forgotten will arise suddenly to consciousness
years later, or, undetected, shape the course of our lives.*

—Susan Griffin, *A Chorus of Stones*

Anna Bertrand,

Cape Town, 2004

'Where is your client, Mr Bellows?'

We are in court, Maria, and Mr Bellows is mopping his balding head with an already damp handkerchief. Even in cold weather he looks hot and moist. Today he also looks embarrassed, like a bulldog that has been caught lifting its leg against the settee.

'I'm not sure, I'm afraid', Bellows admits to the Magistrate. 'I saw him yesterday, and ... he was looking ill, so perhaps he is too indisposed to attend ...' he tries, rather lamely.

'For his sake, I hope he is sufficiently indisposed to be in hospital!' Magistrate Van Deventer is irritated. 'I am revoking bail and sending out an order for his arrest unless you can find him and bring him in by the end of the tea recess.' Mr Bellows lumbers out.

'Next case.' The Magistrate puts Sebastian's case file to one side and nods to the Prosecutor, Nikki. She adjusts the black cape on her shoulders, tucks a frustrated lock of hair behind her ear, and calls the next case.

After tea, Mr Bellows confesses he has not been able to find Sebastian, and the Magistrate postpones the case till next week. We all assume that Sebastian will be arrested in the meantime.

I nod and smile towards Nikki and leave the court.

Later, here in the Archives, I again request Dorothy Feather's file, and find her admission certificate – which a doctor was required to complete in terms of the Lunacy Act of 1891.

MEDICAL CERTIFICATE – THAT A PERSON IS A LUNATIC

I, the undersigned, William Henry Dodds MD, being a duly licensed medical practitioner in this Colony, hereby certify that I, on the 28th day of October 1891 at her father's Residence in Sea Point, personally examined

DOROTHY MARY FEATHER (spinster)
of Spes Bona Villa, Main Road, Sea Point, Cape Town
Occupation: Gentlewoman

and that the said DOROTHY MARY FEATHER is a person of unsound mind, and a proper person to be taken charge of and detained under care and treatment, and that I have formed this opinion upon the following grounds, viz:

Facts indicating Insanity observed by myself:
1) Emaciated, haggard, maniacal
2) Erratic, emotional, very excitable, irresponsible
3) Has erotic hallucinations, is incoherent and
   inconsistent, rambles and mixes fact and fiction
   in her talk.

Facts indicating Insanity communicated to me by others:
Her father assured me that she has recently been rescued from the sea into which she had plunged. Wanders about aimlessly, has her natural affections quite perverted and uses most shameless language when spoken to by her relations. Habitually neglects her person and dresses fantastically.

Signed: William Henry Dodds MD

I cannot imagine what it was like for you, Maria, and for Dorothy – as *proper people to be taken charge of and detained under care and treatment.* What care, what treatment did you get? I have been reading about the state of medicine and psychology in your time, and from these and Dr Dodds' notes in Dorothy's file, I imagine him as some Victorian headmaster trying to correct what was termed 'moral insanity'.

Would a nurse have brought Dorothy to Dr Dodds's consulting rooms for her annual examination and 'treatment'? Did Dodds examine her and pronounce her – as I read in one of his entries in her file – *ill nourished and thin?* He would probably have needed the nurse to hold her still while he examined her because she was, as he put it, *very excitable* and prone to *emotional outbursts.*

He might have tried to talk to her while she rambled incoherently, as he said in the admission certificate, *mixing fact and fiction.* Was she trying to communicate with him, trying to tell him something important in her excitable ramblings? What was it she said that caused him to conclude in her case file: *suffers from Foolish Delusions?*

Each examination report ended with his recommendation that *she continue to be detained in terms of the Lunacy Act,* as she was in his opinion, *still clearly of unsound mind.*

The file is fat with observation notes that cover the 53 years she lived there. The entries describe her slow disintegration from the incessant talking and excitability and 'mania' of the first years, to the 'senile dementia' of her final years when she simply sat staring at her hands, not knowing who or where she was.

From my reading, I learn that the treatment Dr Dodds advocated was something called 'Moral Management', designed to encourage 'good behaviour', described as 'placid, cheerful, co-operative, and diligent'.

I imagine the nurses getting the inmates out of bed in the mornings, and cautioning them to be hard-working and clean and docile if they wanted to be declared *no longer a lunatic,* and allowed back into society where they would continue to work hard, and be clean and docile.

There is no sign that anyone ever visited Dorothy Feather.

Further on in the file I come across a copy of James Feather's will, leaving money in trust: *to my two children, Dorothy and Hester, who to my great sorrow are mentally affected, I leave such sum annually as my trustees and executors may deem necessary for their support, dress and general requirements during their lifetime.*

The night is an empty corridor echoing with the murmurs of ghosts. I lie in the dark, willing death to close over me like a shroud. Beyond this moment is nothing, no hope, no possibility of trying again, no reversing what has happened. I long for oblivion. I ache for release from this frozen body, freedom from this cold place, and from the chill of these memories.

Freedom. Perhaps I am afraid of it, and that is why I cannot die. There was a time when I longed for freedom. I had thought that marrying Trangott would free me from the dullness of my life with Father. And even, perhaps, from behaving and thinking in the way that was expected of a young lady. For Trangott did not seem to care what people thought. He was never wholly comfortable in polite society. I suppose I thought he would allow me a kind of freedom. But his freedom was only for himself, an adventure only for men.

He wanted me where he could find me. Me, his wife, his housekeeper. I had to be there, as the warm centre of his life, and the body in the marriage bed after a frustrating day as Father's store manager. And, of course, as the mother of his children. It was important to Trangott to have a large family. Perhaps to make up for his own lack of family as a child. He had told me of his bleak and solitary childhood in his father's house, with no brothers or sisters, and his father away most of the time. A strict housekeeper was his only company until the age of ten, when he was sent to a military academy. There he stayed until his father died – leaving him enough money to buy his way out of the army and pay for his passage to Cape Town. Like me, he had spent much of his childhood alone in a large, empty house.

It was always quiet and dark when I came back in the afternoons, as if the house had been silently holding its breath from the moment I closed the big door behind me in the morning, until I unlocked it again in the late afternoon.

As soon as I got back I would light the oil lamps and make the fire in the stove. In winter the kitchen was the only warm room in the house. Then I would start supper.

I remember a few years after Mother died, I came home from school and the market later than usual. I walked into the house, put my satchel and the vegetables for the evening meal on the table in the kitchen, and thought I heard Mother calling from upstairs. I started to run up the stairs, eager to see her. But when I reached the top, I remembered. I listened at the landing. Silence. Just the dark house creaking as it cooled down from the day. She was gone, and I was alone in the house. I sat on the top step and wept – for Mother who hadn't meant to die, for myself who was alone in the dark house, and for Father who had become quieter, like the house, and who also creaked in his stiff bones.

Even as a child, I remember Father being an old man. Tall and thin, his hair was already grey at the sides. He had small, round spectacles and he walked with a limp from a childhood injury. I would hear him walking about in the house at night after I went to bed – his uneven scrape-bump, scrape-bump passing my door. He had come out from England to work in his uncle's furniture shop, Bertrand's Quality English Furniture, which he inherited when his uncle died. He imported heavy furniture from England, and sold it to wealthy British people in the Colony.

One Sunday I went to Ouma's for lunch. It was Auntie Dinah's birthday. Father didn't come, but that was not unusual. I gave him lunch early and left him sitting in his big chair, reading the newspaper. I knew he would fall asleep before long, and when I got back I would find him with his head forward, and his spectacles having slipped down his nose. Then I'd make him tea and give him a slice of fruitcake that I would bring back from Ouma's.

Ouma's house was as noisy as Father's was quiet. In Father's house I could hear the clocks ticking. The tall grandfather clock in the hall, the small silver one on the dresser in the dining room, and the grandmother clock in Father's study. If you stood quite still in the passage, in the dead centre of the house, all you could hear were clocks, ticking and chiming.

I stood in the passage that morning, the morning of Auntie Dinah's birthday, listening to the clocks, waiting for all the different chimes to strike the hour. And also listening to Father's movements as he stoked the fire and settled into his chair. Then I quietly left the house.

Ouma had one old clock on the dresser in the kitchen where we usually sat, a brown wooden clock with a big hand that jerked a little when it moved on to the next minute. I often watched it when we sat around the table. Now, in Ouma's kitchen, I looked at the clock, saw it jerking, and listened for its ticking. Nothing. I realised I had never heard it tick. I got up and went over to it and put my ear to its curved polished wood case. I listened. The kitchen was full of people. There was the sound of pans banging as Ouma searched noisily for something in the cupboard. Auntie Dinah was shouting to Thomas to bring her a cloth where baby Andries had spilt his milk. Uncle Bennie was coming in the back door, stamping the dust off his boots. Two neighbours from across the street were holding each other around the waist and singing happy birthday to Auntie Dinah. I couldn't hear the tick of the clock against my ear.

'What is the matter with the clock, child?' asked Ouma, seeing me there, 'Is it broken?'

I shook my head and smiled at her, and then suddenly ran towards her, putting my arms as far around her as they would go, and lay against her. She stroked my hair and I listened to her heart beating beneath my ear.

'Ouma mustn't die,' I pleaded. 'Ouma must never leave this house.' She did die, but much later, just before the twins were born. We called the baby girl Eliza, after her.

When Ouma died, Uncle Bennie took over the house. A carpenter and his wife moved into Ouma's room and a dark man from Grahamstown moved into the shed in the back yard.

It was never the same after she died. That was when I started going to the Café Royal in Church Street whenever Trangott was in one of his moods. It was a peaceful place to escape to, away from Trangott, the guests in the hotel, and even my children. Alone.

Well, I am alone now, really alone, even though I am surrounded by others here in this ward. Alone and trapped in my motionless body and silent voice. It is as if I am holding onto the edge of a deep hole full of memories. Afraid to look down, afraid of seeing the things I have tried so hard to forget. Afraid, too, of remembering the happiness that ended so abruptly, without warning. So I remain in this suspended 'death' and continue to listen to Dorothy's sedated moans.

They brought her back into the day room yesterday, just before supper, her thin shoulders more concave than ever, her hollow eyes staring. She had been locked up all day as punishment for embarrassing Dr Dodds in front of his guests. They put her in the locked gloves, which are supposed to restrain agitated inmates, but have little effect on Dorothy. It is as if her constantly moving hands help to ward off the frightening images in her head, and when she is restrained, the images become more real, and she more frantic.

When they brought her back in, she sidled up to me and sat on the chair next to my wheelchair, whimpering, her fingers pulling at her gown.

'... cloth ... wipe ... torn ... bleeding ... wash cloth ... died ... good girl ... clean ... quiet ... can't tell ... lock up ... bad ...'

Sometimes, when she is more coherent, she tells me about someone dying, but she seems to get confused about whether the person is her, her father, or someone else.

She was so agitated last night that they had to give her a second sleeping draught before we went to bed, but even so, she has been talking now for hours.

I wonder if her father still visits the hotel for his whisky and cigars. I always tried to avoid him if I could. I remember one evening when he arrived earlier than usual. Trangott was busy with a guest in the office, and the other guests had not yet finished dinner. I was clearing dishes when James Feather put his head in at the dining room door and asked me to bring him a whisky. I reluctantly went into the lounge to serve him.

There he was, comfortable as usual, in the red leather armchair, having helped himself to a cigar from Trangott's box in the sideboard drawer. He would have helped himself to whisky, too, I have no doubt, except that he liked to sit back and have it poured and brought to him.

'Hotel full?'

'It will be tomorrow,' I was taken off guard – he did not usually engage me in conversation. 'We're expecting a young Englishwoman to arrive on the ship docking from England.'

'Alone?'

'Yes, she wrote from London. She replied to an

advertisement for a music teacher at Mrs Redfurn's Academy.'

I edged to the door, as fast as politeness allowed. I regretted telling him about her. James Feather had a reputation for pestering young women. I always watched him carefully whenever my daughters were near him, even though I suspected he was afraid of Trangott – of his size and his temper. Rumour had it that Feather was on the lookout for another wife, one that would give him sons.

'What's her name, this young music teacher?' he persisted.

'Miss Booth, I believe.' I was forced to answer, but tried to mumble the name.

He smiled, took a large gulp of his whisky, and leaned back in the chair.

'You may inform Miss Booth that I would be available to introduce her to the city.'

'I doubt she would enjoy visiting the Dance Halls, or frequent the Dock Road Hotel.' I could barely disguise the disdain in my voice.

It was well known that James Feather regularly visited the Dance Halls late at night, especially the one in Chiappini Street where many of the sailors and dockworkers went, as well as a hotel in Dock Road. These were places frequented mostly by rough, single men who drank a great deal, and by prostitutes. No gentlewoman would be seen there.

'You'd be surprised how much young women enjoy what I have to give them.' His small moustache twitched.

I determined to keep Miss Booth out of his way. But as

it turned out, she was destined to come to harm.

Ah. There. Dorothy seems to be falling asleep, though she is still mumbling about death. I wonder if she wants to die – as I do. Two women, tormented by the images in our heads: hers seem to frighten her, while mine give me pain, especially the happy ones. Perhaps she knows I am close to death, and that is why she stays near to me, holds onto me, hoping we will sink into peace together.

Lesson Three – The Presence of the Past

You are of course never yourself.
—Gertrude Stein, *Everybody's Autobiography*

Who is the 'I' of autobiography? Is it the 'I', now, remembering and reflecting on the past, or is it the 'I' we have been – all the 'I's we have been, and even those we might have been? Or, is it, in the end, the 'I' created in words on the page? There are, in fact, three identities in autobiography – the I who lived, the I in the text, and the I who writes *I*.

Then there is the 'eye' of autobiography. As the 'I' who writes about the self, it looks at and sees multiple reflections of our various 'selves' through time and place. Our past selves – and even our future selves – are all present in our 'now' self, our 'writing self'. In looking at our many faces, it is important that our gaze is gentle and steady. Instead of viewing ourselves with harshness or judgment, we need to view those selves with compassion and even humour. In this way, writing autobiography is about self-acceptance.

- *Look at photographs of yourself, past and current, including those which surprise or embarrass you. Create a 'selves-portrait'. Write about what you see, the memories that come from the photographs.*
- *Still looking at the photographs, write about yourself in the third person, using the prompt 'she who ...'*
- *Write about a place that has particular significance for your life – noting the name of the place, the date or age you were, and a colour and an object you associate with the place. Describe a scene, writing in the present tense, and starting with a line of dialogue.*

Anna Bertrand,

Cape Town, 2004

A suitcase full of photographs. I pull it out from under my bed, open
it hesitantly. No order in the suitcase, photos jumbled. Pictures taken
with my brother's Brownie camera, yellow and curling at the edges;
pictures of me as a large-eyed baby held by my mother, as a small
child in a party dress, on a swing, up a tree, one in ballet tunic – my
leg and arm stretched out in an awkward pose. School class photos,
one where you can pick me out from the row of uniformed girls as
the one still in navy blue winter uniform while the rest of the class is
in sky blue summer uniform, my sullen expression a clear indication
that I had forgotten the instruction for the day. Posed photos, three
at dances with young men, an off-the-shoulder dress, my hair (and
expression) blow-dried. A family holiday photo – the five of us under
a beach umbrella on Umkomaas Beach, smiling for the camera,
looking like a toothpaste advertisement. My first ID photo at 16, shy
and innocent. One of me in my twenties, sitting on the steps of the
Johannesburg Library with a girlfriend, cigarette in hand. Photos of
me at protests and marches in the 80s, one holding a banner saying
'Clemency for Sharpeville Six'. Photos of me in graduation gown and
silly flat hat, pulling a face. A recent photo of me sitting at my table
in the front room of my flat, my ginger cat perched on the edge of
my notebook, so that I have to write around him and dodge his lazy
paw as it halfheartedly taps at my pen.

Photos of my mother, father. My father as a young man on a
motorbike before they were married. My mother in her bridal gown

on her wedding day, holding a bouquet of orchids. My father as an old man, gaunt, white-haired, looking disappointed. My mother, grey and stooped, walking with a stick.

Digging through the suitcase, emotionally buffeted by images and memories. Liking some, cringing at others. Hard to see myself as a person separate from the 'me' now. Hard to believe that little girl is me, that awkward schoolgirl, that glamorous date dancing with boys, that one in corduroy trousers and leather jacket, dancing with a girl.

A suitcase full of discarded identities, forgotten selves, selves best ignored. Kept under my bed, next to the suitcase full of discarded clothes. I can't seem to throw the clothes or the photos away.

Opening the suitcase is like when I visit Johannesburg many years after leaving it, finding myself ambushed by the memories of the various periods of my life spread over the different places in the city. As I drive from Johannesburg airport, at one edge of the city, to my mother's retirement village at the other, I cover all the periods of my life, each lived in a different part of the city, all compressed into the space of an hour's drive.

I pass Kensington where I lived in a garden cottage just before I left for Cape Town, and had a secret affair with a married woman. Then Hillbrow where I lived in various flats through the 60s and 70s – the young gay days of clubs and bars, of starting a feminist study and consciousness-raising group, of pavement cafés, talking with friends late into the night, and then walking through the streets of Hillbrow at 2 am to Fontana to buy more cigarettes. After Hillbrow, I pass Wits University where I was a timid and reluctant student, next my high school where I felt safe in my uniform and had my first love affair. Then our suburban home where I spent my childhood, the streets where I rode my bike to school. Then lastly through Melville, and the artist's place I house-sat for a few months, trying to write poetry.

All of my first 36 years of life, squashed into a single hour. A mess of emotions. All of me, none of me. When I came to Cape Town I left them all behind. Yet I brought them with me – in a suitcase now under my bed. While I know they are all me, they also feel like a fiction of me. Perhaps because I was never at home in any of the identities I was trying out.

But now, for the first time in my life, at 56, I feel as if I might find a self I am comfortable with, that suits me.

I push the suitcase back under the bed.

I close my eyes and see the images before me. Images of me, Anna.

She who needs to move and change to get a flow of air around her. She who has a restless spirit, and whose skin prickles, always.

She who lives with her ginger cat, in a flat next to the railway line, and who can see the mountain from her window, and hear the sea on a windless night. She who walks on the beach in the early mornings, loves the sound of gulls and trains and the cello.

She who likes rituals and routine, but needs to break rules, always. She who has never earned much money, who longs to be a writer. She who wears jeans and T-shirts, most of the time, hides behind glasses, has short hair, going grey.

She who has no head for heights but goes out on a limb, anyway.

She who is awkward at social gatherings, who hesitates before hugging a friend, and then bumps clumsily or stands unhugged.

She who is surprised to find she's over 50, already. She who is afraid to be a middle-aged woman, afraid of getting old and frail and stiff like her mother. She who wants to be a boy with dirty knees when she grows up.

She who feels her life is temporary, but who doesn't believe she will die, ever.

She who has difficulty with entrances and exits, always.

—

Cape Town, the city I escaped to – the city with trains, mountains and the sea. I tried out a new 'me' when I moved to Cape Town, twenty years ago. One of my first jobs when I arrived in Cape Town was as a part-time teacher and childcare worker at St Patrick's Boys' Home in the centre of the city.

I am 37, the colour is grey, and the object I see is a filing cabinet.

'Of course, his mother is a lesbian.' Her grey eyes look out from behind her glasses. Her neat grey perm is soft around her kindly face. She talks a lot, with social worker confidence. She knows what she thinks. She knows what is right.

'Here. I'll show you.' She reaches for a file and pages through to a letter with an official State Psychologist letterhead, addressed to her. Her finger pounces onto the third line down – *Jeremy's mother is an active lesbian.*

Jeremy was the first boy I met at the Boys' Home. My first day. I was nervous, sweating into my clean-ironed blouse. Boys everywhere, running, shouting.

'Good afternoon, Miss.' Old world manners, almost a click of heels, open beautiful face, blue innocent eyes, blond hair falling over his forehead, charming, so charming a smile.

'My name is Jeremy Hunt.' His hand in a formal handshake. 'And this is Robert da Silva.'

I shook hands, introduced myself.

'You've come to teach us art?'

'Yes, that as well.'

'Well, I'll be the first one in your class. Hey, Robert? Should we be the first in class?'

Robert mumbled, looked at his feet.

Mrs Brink's sure, manicured finger is still stuck on the third line. I skim-read past ... *mother now living in England, father weak, easily manipulated, married again. Unfortunately stepmother unsympathetic, very strict, tries to control Jeremy, punishes a lot ...* Further down the letter I read the list of things the boy had 'done' to get himself sent here. *An attempted hold-up of the local supermarket with his father's gun, home-made petrol bombs, set fire to a shed* – all by the age of twelve.

I don't really want to know. I had decided that I wanted to form uncluttered relationships with the boys first, afraid that these interpretations from the 'authorities' would interfere with my spontaneous feelings about the boys and the way I interacted with them.

Yesterday I used Mrs Brink's office for Jeremy's extra lesson because there was a meeting in the library.

He had tried to distract me from the lesson as usual.

'My father is one of the richest men in South Africa, you know. My mother – stepmother – has piles and piles of clothes. And I'm going to get two new pairs of shoes when my father comes down to Cape Town. They cost R500 a pair!'

'Wow, that's nice, Jeremy. But come, let's go through your maths for your test tomorrow. OK, what's an acute angle?'

'It's ah … it's um …'

As I watched his eyes, I could see his soul turn its back and run for cover, hide, away from the film of dust that settled around the question. I had lost him again. Change tactic. Remind him that he knows the answer. I drew a circle on the scrap of paper.

'Remember the circle, Jeremy?' Handed him the pencil.

'Oh.' He confidently drew an acute angle, labelled it, smiled like a golden angel, and rattled off the other facts before I could even ask him. I often wondered if his slowness was just a ruse to keep my attention. He so often had moments of clear brilliance. Behind those changeable eyes must be a landscape where everything is known, a world of sharp clarity. Sometimes I'm lucky – when I look into his eyes at the right angle, and catch sight of a tree, a waterfall, a blinding shaft of sunlight. Just now and again.

'Do you come to meetings in this office?'

'No, Jeremy, they have them in the mornings when I'm not here.'

'There's files in there.' His blue eyes looked hard at the filing cabinet.

'Yes.'

'It's locked now.'

'I'm sure.'

'Have you read any of the stuff in there?' Casual.

'No, I'm not interested.'

'Why?' Surprised.

'It's not my business.'

A rare look of trust. 'Have you ever been to a psychologist?'

'No. Never.'

'I have.' Testing.

'Oh? What's it like?'

'Horrible. I'll never go again. They write down everything you say to them and then show it to your father. Get you into trouble.' Still staring at the filing cabinet. 'I'm going to set fire to this place one day.'

I try to read the last few lines as Mrs Brink starts to close the file. *Jeremy has an extremely charming manner, but lives in a world of fantasy.*

The file lands neatly back in its place. Her finger still seems to be pointing. I mentally duck, hoping that this active-lesbian-spotting finger doesn't point in my direction like a divining rod. She turns the key in the filing cabinet.

'Jeremy has always been a real problem at school,' she explains. 'He plays the fool, won't concentrate. Seems to be only interested in girls.'

'Jeremy is a *moffie!* Jeremy is a *moffie!*'

A few weeks ago, three of them were jumping around him like young puppies.

'Did you know that Jeremy is a little bunny rabbit, Miss?'

'Do you want some nice lettuce, *moffie?*'

I tried to look uninterested.

'Ask him where he went after school today, Miss.'

'Ask him why he was late.'

Jeremy looked outraged. 'I played rugby.'

Hoots and jeers. 'You don't play rugby. You don't know how to play rugby.'

'I do. I can prove it.'

'Oh yeah? What position do you play?'

I butt in. 'Listen, this is a homework period. Jeremy is studying. Please keep quiet or go outside.'

Later. At supper. Jeremy on one side of me.

'Would you like some of my Coke, Miss?'

'Don't take it from Jeremy, Miss.'

'Why not?'

Giggle. 'You'll get Aids.'

Jeremy does a rare flare-up. 'You don't know what Aids is.'

'I do.'

'Bet you don't.'

'Bet I do.'

'OK, what is it?'

'It's a disease that makes you a *moffie*.'

Jeremy gives me a what-can-you-say? look.

A year later, Jeremy is now a senior and no longer in my group, but often comes to find me to sit and talk. Always a formal greeting, always a formal leave-taking, and sometimes not much in between.

'Rock Hudson died.'

'Yes, I know.'

'They say he had Aids.'

'Yes.'

Silence.

'What do you get Aids from, Miss?'

'Mainly people get it who have sexual intercourse with someone who has it, and don't use a condom.'

'They say Rock Hudson was gay.'

'Yes, I read that.'

'Oh. Well. Thank you very much, Miss. I must be going now. Have a good evening, Miss.'

A week later. 'I enjoyed our talk last week, Miss.'

'Yes?'

'Funny things we talked about.'

'Anyone else you are wondering about? Anyone giving you problems?' Mrs Brink's kindly eyes wanting to advise, sort out, explain.

'No. No one. I was just worried that Jeremy is going to fail this year.'

'Well, we can't work miracles, you know – what with his background.' She shakes her grey head.

'Yes. Well. Thank you, Mrs Brink. I must go and open up the library. Almost time for study.'

I gather my books from her desk and move towards the door, trying not to walk like an active lesbian.

Dear Maria

Cape Town is a special city for me. Made even more special now, knowing you once lived here too. Today, I walked up Adderley Street from the station, and passed the Standard Bank, which was built in 1882 – its dome above the columns and pediments surmounted by the figure of Britannia. I turned into Shortmarket Street and walked through Greenmarket Square, bordered by the Old Town House and Central Methodist Church. And it was as if these cobbles and grand old buildings still contained the spirit of your Cape Town. I had a deep sense of the presence of the past, here in the same buildings and streets of over a century ago.

I walked up Long Street to the corner of Church Street, and stood there, looking at a square flat-roofed, two-storey building. It is now called Scott House, but it used to be the Germania Hotel. Your Germania Hotel, Maria. How did I discover that this was the hotel that you and Trangott once owned? Well, I came across it in the Cape Almanac of 1883. Looking under 'Hotels', I found: *Germania Hotel, proprietor T Schultz, 64 Church Street, c/r Long.* Then a visit to the Deeds Office to check the erf number, and there it was – the same building you lived in over 100 years ago, still standing, still with a rickety staircase going up to the first and second floors. It's now a mixture of antique shop, junk shop, some poky offices, and a gallery upstairs.

I noticed, too, in the Cape Almanac that your neighbours in Long Street were Miss Dryer, milliner; A Boyes, boot and shoemaker; and Ward & Co, saddler. And your neighbours on the other side: R Taylor, grocer; I Waldegrave, harness maker and JH Youle, cutler. What is a cutler? A maker of cutlery? And then there was a Mrs Mackay, who had a private boarding house on the next corner at 58 Long Street. She had a display advert in the Cape Almanac. As did the Café Royal, which advertised an *Upstairs Ladies Room* which was *replete with every convenience.*

I remember the Café Royal in Church Street. It was the oldest pub in Cape Town, but was gutted by fire a few years ago, and recently demolished. Did you ever go there? Were you one of the 'Ladies' who frequented the Upstairs Ladies Room?

:30   ADVERTISEMENTS.

CAFE ROYAL
GRILL ROOM & RESTAURANT,
NO. 9, CHURCH STREET,
NEXT DOOR TO GENERAL POST OFFICE.

THE JAPANESE LUNCHEON BAR.

The most Elegant and best appointed Room of its class in South Africa.

THE SMOKING ROOM.

The place to spend a few minutes' Lounge, supplied with Writing Table, &c. and all the principal English, Scotch and Colonial Papers and Directories.

THE BILLIARD ROOM.

THE BEST IN CAPE TOWN.

THE DINING ROOM.

ONE OF THE FINEST DINING ROOMS IN THE CITY.

Commercial Dinner à la Carte at separate Tables, every day from 12 to 3 o'clock. This Room is admirably adapted for the use of Private Dinner Parties, &c.

THE LADIES' ROOM

Is Upstairs, and will be found replete with every convenience.

Private Entrance to Ladies' Room and Dining Rooms, Lavatories, &c.

WINES & SPIRITS OF THE BEST QUALITY,

ALE AND STOUT ON DRAUGHT.

CHARGES MODERATE.

Large Public Banquets, Luncheons, Dinners, Soirees, Balls, &c., Catered for in first-class style.

Arrangements made for Private Luncheons, Dinners, Suppers, &c.

JOHN DUNN, Proprietor.

Just off the corner of Church Street is the Café Mozart, my inner-city sanctuary, with its own upstairs room. The building is as old as your Germania across the road, and probably as old as the Café Royal.

As I climbed the steep, narrow steps of the old wooden staircase at Café Mozart this morning, and sat at my usual window table, I imagined that I was in the Café Royal, looking down at the street below – the same street you would have walked along a century or more ago. Today it is a pedestrian mall, closed to cars, with café tables, stalls selling antiques and bric-a-brac, and hawkers, street musicians and tourists. I could see the balcony of your Germania Hotel, and I imagined I was in the Upstairs Ladies Room at the Café Royal, looking down at horse carriages, ladies in long dresses, and washerwomen carrying bundles of laundry.

The weather probably hasn't changed much – cold, wet winters, drizzly days like today when you might have come, as I have, to relax and be warm and comfortable.

There is seldom anyone else up here, other customers tend to sit companionably downstairs or in the shade of the umbrellas outside. Today, though, a woman about my age sat at a table opposite me, at the other window overlooking Church Street, reading a letter. I found myself staring at her – she seemed strangely familiar. She ordered a pot of tea and lingered over it. She kept looking up from her letter – at the top of the stairs, or out the window – as if expecting to see someone. She wore a long dress with a high collar, rather like the clothes you would have worn. In fact, I started to imagine she was you. I liked the look of her. A quiet, centred manner, even though she seemed to be waiting for someone who did not arrive. Her hands were strong and sure as she poured the tea. Her face as I imagine yours to have been – open, gentle, and serene. But you could never have looked like this, I decided, not with six children and a hotel to run.

Suddenly, the woman seemed to decide to leave. She called the waiter, paid, picked up her umbrella, and went down the stairs. Spontaneously, I decided to follow her. I left money on the table and followed her down the staircase, and out the door. It was raining lightly but I didn't want to stop to put on my raincoat in case I lost sight of her. She was waiting to cross Long Street. I held back as she crossed, so she wouldn't see me. A newspaper van went past, and by the time I got across, she had vanished. She was nowhere to be seen along Church Street or on either side of Long Street. I decided she must have gone into a shop.

I was standing outside the old Germania. Could she possibly have gone in there? I looked through the window into the antique shop – no sign of her – then into the junk shop, then peered up the rickety staircase leading to the first floor and the art gallery. I wondered about going up, when a man's voice behind me said, 'Excuse me, please.' I turned to see a large man with a square head and a heavy moustache behind me. 'You look for someone?' he asked in a strong German accent. Before I could answer, the woman I had been following appeared at the top of the stairs. She stared at me and I could see she recognised me from the restaurant. She seemed disconcerted at the sight of me and looked inquiringly at the man. 'No,' I said. 'Sorry, excuse me ...' and I moved out of his way. He walked up the stairs to join the woman.

circle four

INVENTING THE TRUTH

Making things up and fact are two different things,
but you may need some of both to get to the truth.

—Toni Morrison, quoted by Tristine Rainer, *Your Life as Story*

£25 REWARD

*Mysterious Disappearance
of a Young Lady*

Left her Residence on Thursday Afternoon, 24st inst. – A YOUNG LADY, about 19 years of age, tall and very slight; features regular and rather long, complexion rather pale and delicate; hair, dull golden; dressed in blue print dress, with white ring pattern; white hat with ostrich feather. Had with her a sunshade of green shot silk.

Anyone seeing a Lady answering to the above description is requested to induce her to return to the undernoted Address, where all information will be thankfully received. Twenty-five Pounds Reward will be given for information which shall lead to her recovery.

MRS PFAFF,
Hope Mill, top of the Avenue,
Cape Town.

Information may also be lodged
at the Police Stations,
Cape Town and Sea Point.

£25 REWARD.

Mysterious Disappearance of a Young Lady.

LEFT her Residence on Thursday Afternoon, 24th inst., —A YOUNG LADY, about 19 years of age, tall and very slight ; features regular and rather long, complexion rather pale and delicate ; hair, dull golden ; dressed in blue print dress, with white ring pattern ; white hat with ostrich feather. Had with her a sunshade of green shot silk.

Anyone seeing a Lady answering to the above description is requested to induce her to return to the undernoted Address, where all information will be thankfully received. Twenty-five Pounds Reward will be given for information which shall lead to her recovery.

MRS. PFAFF,
Hope Mill, top of the Avenue,
Cape Town.

Information may also be lodged at the Police-stations, Cape Town and Sea Point.

Anna Bertrand,

Cape Town, 2004

Dear Maria

Yesterday, in the South African Library, I came across an advertisement placed in the *Cape Times* on 27 May 1889. I was scrolling through old newspapers from your time, trying to immerse myself in the spirit of your era, trying to get a sense of the mood, concerns and language of the past, to transport myself back into the Cape Town of the late 1880s, your Cape Town.

I'd never been particularly interested in history, or historical detail until I 'met' you. But now I find myself obsessed by the need to know more, to find my way through the fog of the past 100 years.

By looking at old photographs, old newspapers, by reading letters and journals written by people who lived at the same time as you, a picture starts emerging, slowly at first, and then gradually becoming clearer. It is like the process of watching a photograph develop in a darkroom. At first there is just the sheet of blank white paper submerged in a basin of chemicals. Then slowly, magically, with increasing sharpness, a picture comes to life.

So, too, with your Cape Town and your life, Maria. I find this advertisement, and start to see her, this tall, slight, pale young lady with her blue print dress and white hat, carrying a sunshade of green shot silk.

And I wonder ... was she ever found and 'induced to return' to Mrs Pfaff?

Some nights my thoughts and memories are as lifeless and numb as my body. But tonight the memories come rolling into shore on waves of smells, sounds and even tastes.

Tonight, I could be waiting for an omnibus in Adderley Street, as the stagnant smell of the *grachts* after the rains mixes with the smell of horse manure as wagons and carriages pass down the street, and with the smell of oil from the street lamps and smoke from the chimneys. There are smells from the houses as people prepare their evening meals. And now a wave of smells from our hotel kitchen hits me. Soup simmering on the stove, coffee, and Lizzie's spicy *bredie* and *bobotie*. And, mingled with these, the smoky smell from our old coal stove.

Other smells. The smell of Trangott as he noisily came to bed at night – a mixture of sweat, cigars and whisky – as he sat heavily on the bed, tugged at his boots, and let them fall with a thud on the floor.

On washdays there was the smell of freshly-laundered sheets and towels drying next to the stove. The smell of freshly-bathed children on bath days. On Saturday mornings Lizzie and I would put the big iron tub in the kitchen and boil kettles on the stove. The children gathered around, waiting their turn, shivering and complaining in winter when the kitchen windows fogged over.

We bathed the youngest first. Always, it seemed, there was a baby who had to be dipped in the warm, soapy water before being rinsed and handed to Lizzie or an older child to be dried with a towel warmed near the stove. Then, more water was poured into the tub as the older children took turns to be scrubbed and rinsed before drying themselves and dressing in front of the stove.

Lizzie and I usually bathed at night, after the children were in bed and we had cleaned the kitchen after dinner. Occasionally, Trangott would chase everyone out of the kitchen and take a bath, but generally he chose to go to the Long Street Baths once or twice a week.

Trangott seemed to be constructed from square blocks – his head, his neck, and even his full beard, which he trimmed to the shape of his square jaw. His wide, square shoulders and huge, muscular arms ended in square hands. Even his calves looked square. And with his German accent, square words seemed to come out of his mouth.

Soon after I met Trangott, I took him to Ouma's house for Sunday lunch. He had to stoop to get through the front door, and turned sideways to pass through the hall with its hat-stand. When he shook Uncle Bennie's hand I saw it disappear into Trangott's hand, trapped by those square fingers. After lunch, Trangott sank into the sofa in the sitting-room, trying, I think, to look less imposing. He also tried to be charming. And he was, in his way.

I could see Ouma liked him, even though I suspect she

would have preferred me to marry one of the local boys. But Trangott's energy appealed to her. It was so different from Father's. I think she responded to his warmth as he played with cousin Jan's two-year-old who tried to climb up his legs as if they were tree trunks. Trangott bellowed his large laugh and swung the child up onto his lap and let her pull his beard for the rest of the afternoon.

'He's not bad for an *uitlander*,' she whispered to me in the kitchen when I went to help her with the dishes, 'and he is good with children. I think he is a good man, and you will know he is there, not like your father. You could do worse, my child.' I took this as her blessing.

Years later, after the birth of John, Hermann and Bertha, Ouma witnessed Trangott's temper for the first time. She had come with Lizzie to bring the laundry, and she walked into the kitchen as Trangott came in from the back yard.

'Who broke my fishing rod?' he shouted, his face red and looking twice its size. He was holding half the fishing rod in one hand and waving the other half around, knocking a pot off the stove as he did so.

My eldest, John, piped up. 'It was Hermann. He was practising casting a line and it caught in the washline. He tried to get it loose and broke it.'

Hermann began to cry and ran behind Ouma's wide skirt. Trangott stood in front of Ouma, breathing hard and waving the piece of fishing rod. She stood her ground, staring calmly at him.

'Leave him, Trangott,' she said with the firm voice she always used with Father. 'He is a little child and it was an accident.'

Trangott spluttered, seemed to consider pushing her out of the way, and then decided against it. He let out a low growl and strode out of the kitchen.

Ouma sat down heavily at the kitchen table, and I could see she was not as calm as she had appeared to be with Trangott. 'A bad, bad temper, my child,' she said, comforting Hermann who had crawled whimpering onto her lap.

'I ignore him, Ouma, when he is angry. Usually, he shouts for a while, sometimes smashes something, and then goes for a long walk, I think to the tavern, and comes back rather drunk, but improved. And he apologises to me afterwards. It is as if his father, the General, is inside him and suddenly takes over, frightening and bullying everyone around him. Afterwards he is sorry and tries to make it up to the children. He tells me he hates to see them as frightened of him as he used to be of his father.'

'Bad, bad temper,' she continued to mutter to herself.

The children all grew up wary of Trangott's temper. But they loved his good moods.

'Come. We all go to the Company Gardens for a picnic,' he would say at these times, and I packed a picnic basket, gathered hats and coats, and the whole family set off up Adderley Street to the Company Gardens. There, Trangott played with the boys, John, Hermann and Gottlieb, and even let Bertha and Eliza join in some of the games. While I, holding baby Georgina, spread a blanket on the grass and watched my family enjoying themselves.

But Trangott's happy moods became less and less frequent as time went by, and later it was only the older children who could remember the picnics in the Company Gardens.

Lesson Four – Inventing the Truth

In the text, as in dreams, there is no entrance. I offer this as a test to all apprentice-writers: if you are marking time you are not yet there. In the text, as in the dream, you're right there.

—Heléne Cixous, *Three Steps on the Ladder of Writing*

The term 'auto/biography' challenges conventional notions of fact and truth in autobiography. Liz Stanley explains: 'Within this sort of autobiography, fact and fiction, fantasy and reality, self and others intermingle in ways that encourage active readership.'

Writing accurate facts is not the same as writing the truth. It can be more 'true' to write that you are lost in a strange place searching for a crocodile, or that you are swimming in a pool with no water, than to make sure you have the correct name of your high school science teacher or the exact year you started to wear glasses. What matters is emotional truth, not factual or literal truth.

In dreams we touch the essence of our emotions, the essence of fear, helplessness, freedom, tenderness, rage. So, too, in writing. Remembering and dreaming are simply different forms of imagining. We need to write like we dream, to move below the surface. To do this, we may need to change the facts or sequence of events, invent the dialogue, change the ending – and so capture the emotional truth of a particular time, relationship, or situation.

- *Describe a dream – possibly a recurring dream. Show how the dream reality contrasts with your everyday reality.*
- *Create a scene in which you allow your imagination to 'invent the truth' of an ancestor's life.*

Anna Bertrand,
Cape Town, 2004

I wake to the sound of the first train of the day which hoots as it passes my window and stops with a squeal of wheels at False Bay Station, just 100 metres from my flat. I stare into the dark, the street lamps outside casting a dim light through the window.

My cat, lying against my legs, yawns and stretches his golden body, loosening his curled-up pose of the night. I echo him – yawning and stretching my body, too, stiff from the long night and from accommodating the cat who objects to being disturbed. I dislodge him, and he jumps from the end of the bed onto the window sill, where he stares out at the still-dark morning.

I throw off the duvet, forcing myself to leave the cosiness of the bed, then swing my legs over the side, and slide my feet into the slippers on the floor. I sit a moment, feeling the stiffness of my body, and resolve to start the yoga classes – details of which I have pinned up on my notice-board together with the article describing the benefit of yoga for women in menopause.

I hear the first hesitant chirps of the birds in the tall palm trees on the other side of the railway line. I look around my flat – its bare white walls and my few items of furniture giving off a quiet simplicity. When I moved from Johannesburg to Cape Town, I left behind all my furniture and most of my things. I brought only books – boxes and boxes of them – some clothes, and of course my suitcase of photographs.

I feel the sharp winter air pierce my pyjamas, and I pull a jersey over my head as I pad to the bathroom, pausing on the way to switch on the kettle in the alcove that functions as a kitchenette. I make my tea and carry the cup back to the bed, picking up my notebook and pen from the table. I prop myself up on my pillows and stare out of the window. As I sip my tea, I watch the gradual lightening of the sky and the slow emergence of the mountain. The sunrise colours the rocks on the slopes of the mountain, and, like the bits of cloud drifting by, wisps of a dream come into my mind. I try to capture them in my notebook.

Another 'lost' dream. What 'lost' place this time? A strange city, late at night, setting off from somewhere, a party or a conference? I have to get back to ... where? a hotel, somewhere on the other side of town. I don't know the way, no map, no directions.

It is dark, the streets are deserted. For some reason, my feet are bare, the pavement hard and cold beneath them. I walk through a deserted industrial area – warehouses, high fences, large trucks and heavy machinery. No one else around. I keep walking, hoping I am going in the right direction.

A figure approaches – a man in a creased suit – weaving and staggering a little. I cross to the other side of the road. He calls out to me as I pass him, but I don't respond.

It starts to get light. The industrial area now becomes a residential area, small box-like houses with neat front lawns, children in school uniform waiting in driveways for parents to take them to school.

I pass the houses, feeling grubby after my night walk. I turn a corner and see a bus stop ahead. I join the short queue, and stand behind a large, well-dressed woman, whose slightly swollen feet bulge over her sandals. I want to ask her if she knows where the hotel district is, but I can't seem to find my voice. I try clearing my throat.

The woman turns and stares at me with a strange expression on her face – a mixture of horror and amusement. I glance down at my body, wondering if my clothes are dirty, and see that I am naked. Completely.

What has happened to my clothes? Surely I haven't been walking through the streets all this time with no clothes on? I stare down – at my naked breasts, my rounded stomach. Very rounded. Too rounded. I look pregnant. Am I pregnant? How can I be pregnant? I try to reassure myself that this might just be a dream.

I have never been pregnant before, so how would I know if this is pregnant? Do I feel pregnant? My belly feels very heavy. Maybe this woman at the bus stop will know whether I am pregnant. I try to ask her, but I still have no voice. She turns away from me, shaking her head.

The bus arrives, stops at the bus stop. People start to get in. I can't decide what to do. Will the driver allow me to board? A pale, middle-aged naked woman with a bulging belly? What about sitting next to someone – someone all dressed up in their work clothes, smelling of deodorant or hairspray or aftershave?

The plump feet of the woman in front of me start to climb the steps into the bus. I do not move. The busdriver looks past the woman, then starts to close the door of the bus. He doesn't appear to see me standing there. Am I invisible? The plump-footed woman *looked at me, but the busdriver stared straight through me.*

I tell myself I am lucky – now that I am invisible – because no one will see that I am naked. But somehow it feels worse to be invisible. How can I find my way if I am invisible? And what about being pregnant? Can an invisible person be pregnant?

I wake to the sound of the first train of the morning.

Valkenberg Asylum,
Sunday 22 June 1894

I fold my story around myself. I fold my story to protect what I had, what I lost, as a caterpillar binds a cocoon around itself, appearing to be dead. But it waits, waits till the time comes for it to transform itself – for its story to unfold.

My story! Each of the others will have their versions of the story. Trangott had his, the police had theirs, and the children, poor souls, will have theirs. Will they tell these to each other, or retreat in confusion? All their lives I protected them, lulling them into a false sense of a safe world. And then I shattered it, leaving them out in the world, unprotected. I hope that the older ones are comforting the younger three – Georgina, only fifteen, and the twins barely nineteen. They are too young to be left without parents.

Nineteen. The same age as that girl, Emily Booth, who disappeared. The one Mrs Pfaff tried to help, who stayed one night at our hotel before going on to Mrs Redfurn's Academy. She had come out from England as a music teacher for the Academy, she thought. But instead she found herself employed as a servant, and she didn't settle at all. Perhaps they worked her too hard, paid her too little, and there was even talk that Mr Redfurn was rather too free with his hands. Emily Booth eventually ran away.

One night, while involved in her rescue mission for 'decent English girls', Mrs Pfaff found Emily working as a prostitute at the Dock Road Hotel. Mrs Pfaff was a wealthy widow who travelled around Cape Town in her carriage each night, going into taverns, hotels and even brothels to persuade the girls to come back to her large house in Oranjezicht which she had converted into a safe refuge for young women.

Many of the girls Mrs Pfaff rescued had come out from England and Europe with the promise of work in respectable wealthy homes or perhaps even the prospect of marriage to a merchant. Many, like Emily Booth, ended up as badly paid servants, often abused by their employers, and forced to turn to prostitution.

Emily had seemed happy and grateful to stay with Mrs Pfaff, and spoke of trying to find a position teaching music. She promised Mrs Pfaff she would never go near Dock Road again. But two days later she disappeared, and Mrs Pfaff put advertisements in the newspapers.

I went to see Mrs Pfaff a few days after Emily's disappearance to see if there was anything I could do to help.

'What do you think happened?' I asked. 'Do you think she ran away?'

'No, she left all her belongings behind. They are all in her room still – she must have intended to come back here. The police are looking for her everywhere, from Wynberg to Sea Point. And I have been to Dock Road every night in case she decided to go back there, or at least to find out if any of the women there had seen her. I don't know where else to look. The police say they are going to raid the brothels tonight – they may perhaps find her there.'

Emily was found by the police the next day. Dead. Washed up on the rocks at Queen's Beach in Sea Point. She had been raped and strangled.

Mrs Pfaff was inconsolable. 'That poor innocent girl. It is the worst thing that has ever happened to one of my girls. I will not rest until that depraved monster is found.'

'Do you think it might be the same man who killed that young woman in Barrack Street last month?' I later asked Sergeant de Bruin who was investigating the case. Auntie Dinah had told me about her neighbour's daughter who was working at 52 Barrack Street, a well-known brothel. She had been raped and strangled on her way home.

But Sergeant de Bruin did not think so. 'This one was a proper European lady,' he explained 'not a *Hottentot meid* like the other one.'

I wondered what he might think of me if I weren't married to Trangott, and light-skinned enough to pass for a 'proper European lady'. Or of my mother, who was a *'Hottentot meid'* from Constitution Street. I had inherited my father's pale English complexion rather than Mother's dark skin. Father was apparently unconcerned about Mother's 'coloured' background. Ouma had told me the story of how my mother met Father. She was working at Solomon's Bakery in Shortmarket Street, and Father, a shy young Englishman, used to come in every day to buy bread. After many months, they struck up a friendship, and then quite abruptly he asked her to marry him. She just laughed at first, but he refused to give up, and slowly she grew to know him and trust him.

'He is not an easy man,' she told Ouma, 'but he has a kind heart and he doesn't drink or gamble.'

He was quite a few years older than she was, and owned property and a thriving business. But his silence and the oppressiveness of the dark house eventually weighed her down, Ouma said, 'That is why she was so pleased when you were born – there was some life in the house.' I think Father must have loved her in his pale way, because he became even quieter after she died, seldom went out, and never showed any interest in any other woman.

Father died during the fever epidemic of 1882.

I remember that day. Hermann and the twins were also ill, but not as ill as Father. I spent the night running between the children upstairs and Father downstairs – wiping Father with a cool cloth, trying to keep his fever down, then hearing Eliza cough, back upstairs, then a rub for her chest, sitting with her until she fell asleep, watching her, her mouth slightly open, breathing hoarsely, a slight tremor in her breath. She was like her grandfather, pale and delicate. It was the sturdy ones, those who took after Trangott, who withstood the fever best – Bertha and Gottlieb. Their strong, thickset bodies were a good match for the sickness that was fast spreading through Cape Town. The hospitals were full, and the doctors were working late and long hours, treating the sick and the dying.

I sat on the chair next to Father's bed, mopping his

forehead. I knew he was dying. I could feel him drifting, pulling away. His cheeks were grey and dull, as if death had already taken charge of him, deep inside his body, and was now working its way to the surface. His eyes, never fully alive, stared dully out of his bony face, seeming to look at something beyond me. His breath rasped.

I had thought of sending for Dr Hawkins again, but knew that he was either out attending to others or had managed to get home for a few hours sleep. I would do what I could to keep Father comfortable, but no one could stop this creeping, cold death.

I had still not slept when the morning light pushed through the kitchen window and Trangott came downstairs. He washed in the tub I had prepared for him. The contrast between his fleshy body and Father's bony frame struck me, as Trangott stripped to the waist and washed himself noisily, splashing soapy water over the kitchen floor. Father had always bathed in his room. I would leave the basin of hot water outside his door and he returned it for me or Lizzy to empty, without leaving a drop on the floor for us to mop up.

This morning Trangott finished drying himself and dressing, and sat down heavily at the table. I poured his coffee and put a plate of bread and sausage in front of him.

'How is your father?' he asked without looking up.

'He is not well – I thought he would die in the night.'

'I will go past Dr Hawkins on my way to the shop, and ask him to come again.'

'Thank you.' I filled his cup once more.

'Has Hermann come down?'

'He is still ill, too weak to go to the shop.'

Trangott swore. 'What about Bertha?'

'She must go to school.'

'Not today, I need her in the shop, there is a new shipment today, and with your father not there …'

He finished his bread, drained his coffee, and wiped his mouth with the back of his hand.

'Send her over before nine.'

I heard the front door slam behind him.

Father died late that afternoon. Dr Hawkins arrived in time to declare him dead from the fever.

The funeral was a dull, quiet affair, with only my family, a few neighbours, and my cousins from Constitution Street. Trangott cleared Father's room the next day, and he and I moved downstairs, giving the children more space, and saving Trangott the climb up the staircase.

It was not even two months later that Trangott announced to us at dinner that he would be selling the furniture business and turning the shop and warehouse into a hotel. 'Plenty of Germans are coming to Cape Town, they need somewhere to stay, good German cooking. We will call it "The Germania". John and Hermann will help me with the running of the hotel, and you and Bertha will do the cooking and cleaning.'

And so it happened. Though I did insist that Trangott continue to employ Lizzie and that he hire a cleaning woman for the linen and kitchen duties, so that Bertha could continue attending school.

Of all the children, John missed Father the most. In the evenings they used to sit in Father's room and read the newspaper together, like two elderly gentlemen. Father was in his 70s, and fifteen-year-old John looked like a smaller version of him. How careful parents have to be about names. Could it be that by naming our first born after Father, John was destined to be a copy of him?

Hermann, our second child, was named after Trangott's grandfather, who died in Germany when Trangott was still a child. How much Hermann was like his great-grandfather I'll never know, but he was a sensitive boy, and sociable, always keen to visit his cousins and Ouma in Constitution Street. Whenever we visited, he spent the time playing with the children in the street. He was thin and dark and seemed to have inherited none of Trangott's looks or temperament.

Bertha, our third child, was named after Trangott's mother who had died in childbirth. She was the cleverest of the three older children, and I was determined to keep her at school and out of the hotel. I wanted her to have the chance at least of being an independent woman – a teacher perhaps, as I had wanted to be.

It was after Bertha's birth that I started to have problems with my pregnancies and subsequent childbirths. I lost a lot of blood when Bertha was born, and was not well for weeks afterwards. As a result, Dr Hawkins was concerned about my having more children. But Trangott insisted on having a large family. 'My security,' he said. Some women seemed to manage to avoid their husband's demands at certain times of the month and did not get pregnant, but I was ignorant and therefore unfortunate. And Trangott ignored my pleas. 'You are my wife. It is your duty,' he told me.

The twins, Gottlieb and Eliza, were born. For two days afterwards, the midwife thought I might die. Again, Trangott was not prepared to listen to Dr Hawkins' warnings. And not long afterwards I had another daughter, Georgina. The next two pregnancies resulted in miscarriages. Then, after the second miscarriage, my body seemed to take charge of itself, and I bore no more children. Trangott blamed me for the miscarriages. 'It is because you did not want it,' he raged. He would not speak to me for several weeks afterwards – leaving me to deal with my grief on my own.

Anna Bertrand,

Cape Town, 2004

Dear Maria

It is just before 7 o'clock on a winter's morning. I am sitting on a cold stone bench in a courtyard in the garden of Valkenberg Hospital, looking up at this old building, now neglected, paint peeling, boarded-up windows, damp creeping up from the ground. It is still quite dark. The trees are large and loom over the top of the roof, its chipped tiles faded to a dull red. The broken gutters are heavy with sodden old leaves, and the old wooden floorboards of the stoep are stained and cracked.

I came here this morning because I want to be close to you, to feel what you felt on a cold winter morning in June. It is as if this building still holds the memories, the presence, of the time you and Dorothy Feather shared a ward behind these windows.

Some parts of this huge building are still used, mostly as storage and offices for the Friends of Valkenberg. And the adjoining building still operates as a ward, it is still the women's section. I know this because I came last week to talk to the Friends of Valkenberg, offering to do voluntary work for them. A nice woman offered me filing, which I refused, or to help with her weekly hairdressing salon where women patients come to have their hair done. She thinks there is 'no better therapy for these poor women than to feel they look pretty.' She's probably right.

I talked my way around the sleepy guard at the gate this morning, telling him I was a Friend of Valkenberg. And when I leave, he will ask me to open the boot of my car as he has done before. Does he suspect that people smuggle out patients? I wish I might smuggle you and Dorothy, to freedom.

There's no one else around yet.

Sitting on this old stone bench that was surely here in your time, Maria, I search to find your story. Here, in the garden, where the unpruned rose bushes have grown woody, their scent no longer wafting through the barred windows of the ward I decide was surely yours.

Can you hear me, Maria, as you lie there, waiting for daylight and the first bird call?

I am trying to write about myself, to be honest and truthful, trying to go below the surface, to reveal the truth about myself. And I find I am afraid. Afraid of being vulnerable. Afraid of opening myself, of exploring places inside myself and then baring those places, in words on the page, for others to read. Afraid of drawing a reader into my dark places, afraid of the touch on my naked skin.

I had a dream once, where I woke up one morning to find I had no skin – my raw flesh was exposed. No one around me seemed to notice, and people reached out to me. I shrank from their touch, which I knew would be searingly painful. Writing below the surface feels like being skinless. I hold back, from the intimate touch of a reader, and even from intimacy with myself.

But it seems easier to be truthful when I write to you, Maria. To the 'you' inside me. I escape into your story and find I can tell the truth about myself. Hidden in your story, I show myself through you, visible only through you. Finding my way into my own truth through you, I am able to go below the dry leaves of my ordinary life, to the place of the 'un-lie', the damp, mouldy, dark mulch, where the leaves lose their edges, their separateness, and merge in a warm, steamy heap. This is the place where your story resounds in me. I hear it in my heartbeat, feel it moving through my bloodstream.

By writing to you, dear great-grandmother, I reach deep inside and outside at the same time.

Did you have anyone to listen to you? Did you have friends? Did you have any time for friends, with your six children, seeing to Trangott's needs, and helping to run the hotel? Did you read and discuss things – newspapers, books? Did you read Olive Schreiner's *Story of an African Farm*, which was published in 1883? I read recently that her book was one of the catalysts that lead to the formation of the Women's Christian Temperance Union – the women's organisation that eventually pressed for women's suffrage in South Africa.

Perhaps you met Olive Schreiner after she returned to South Africa in 1889? She lived in the small Karoo village of Matjesfontein, but visited Cape Town from time to time. Her letters show that she stayed with her brother, Will, at his house in Hof Street, in Gardens, or else at a boarding house in Cape Town. I wonder whether this may have been the boarding house run by Mrs Mackay, your neighbour, in Long Street?

It was in Matjesfontein that Olive Schreiner wrote *Dreams*, published in 1890 by Fisher Unwin, and sold at two shillings a copy. Did you buy a copy? You may even have discussed it with Olive Schreiner herself, or with a friend, in the Upstairs Ladies Room of the Café Royal.

I try to imagine your life, and feel overwhelmed. I think of trying to run a hotel in times when there was no water laid on, no electricity, and everyone wore elaborate, white clothes that needed starching and ironing. Not to mention the hotel linen, and making sure that clothes for six children were clean. What did you do in winter, like now, when nothing dries in Cape Town and it often rains for weeks on end?

I don't think I could have coped without the support of a friend. When I was reading up on the Women's Christian Temperance Union, I came across a list of names of prominent members. Were any of them your friends? There was one name on the list that looked familiar – Rebecca Melrose. Why the name is familiar, I don't know, but I'm sure I've seen it somewhere recently.

Emily Booth's rape and murder was the catalyst that brought the women of Cape Town together and started our Women's Union.

Soon after the murder, Mrs Mary Leavitt of Cleveland, Ohio, came to South Africa on her world tour. Many of us went to hear her talk, and we formed the first Cape Town branch of the Women's Christian Temperance Union. I joined the Union, interested especially in the vote for women, and legislation affecting women and children. I enjoyed being amongst like-minded women, who were concerned about the same issues as I was.

I had, in fact, been working on these issues on my own for some years. My 'work' started one Saturday morning. Trangott decided to take us all on the inaugural train trip from Cape Town station to Kalk Bay. The line had until then only gone as far as Wynberg, but it had just been extended, and tickets were being offered for the first trip.

We set off, walking down Long Street towards the station – Trangott striding in front, then the older boys, John and Hermann, in their smart suits and new boots. John in his new waistcoat was walking proudly behind Trangott, while Hermann already looked untidy, and was kicking at stones in the street. Bertha, with her bonnet tied under her chin, was next, with a twin on either side – Gottlieb's fat little hand in hers, while Eliza held onto her skirts. Georgina and I were behind with the lunch basket.

I hoped Trangott would not spoil the day by complaining about the dirt in the street. The day before he had shown me a letter in *The Lantern* written by a visitor from England, a doctor, saying the conditions in Cape Town were unhealthy, and warning about another outbreak of smallpox. The letter described what the doctor called 'moral degradation', mentioning that there were over 150 places in Cape Town that sold liquor. He also complained about the prostitution, and the drunkenness of the 'coloureds' and 'kaffirs'; and about the squatters above the Roeland Jail, 'living like animals in holes', and the many who lived on the streets, and slept in doorways.

'What can people do if they are poor?' I had argued with Trangott. 'We are lucky, we have a house and food. The children never go to bed hungry.'

'It is because I work for it, and do not lie around drunk and dirty in the street. I am a respectable businessman.'

Yes, thanks to my father, I thought to myself.

That morning, on the way to the station, we passed a woman and her young daughter sitting on the steps of the Central Methodist Church in Greenmarket Square, thawing their thin bodies in the early morning sun. Their clothes were torn and dirty. The girl looked about ten years old, just a year or two younger than my Bertha.

I knew what would soon happen to this poor young girl,

and might even have happened already. A man would come staggering down Long Street after drinking all night in a tavern. She would be raped in exchange for a few pennies to buy food, and probably also liquor for her mother. The worst aspect was that even if the police saw and arrested the man, there would be no repercussions if the girl was ten years old, the legal age of consent. The law was on his side.

I wanted to stop and ask the woman if she knew about the Refuge in Keerom Street, but Trangott was striding ahead and would be angry to see me talking to 'rubbish' in the street. I promised myself I would go back the next day and find the woman and child and take them to the Refuge – a place of safety run by a group of Anglican nuns for prostitutes who wished to escape the streets, and young servant girls without families who had fallen pregnant, often as a result of rape or prostitution.

At the station I held tightly onto Georgina's hand as we pushed our way through the crowd. We found a carriage, and had only just settled in when the train hooted and shuddered and we were off.

I did go down to Greenmarket Square the next morning, but the mother and child were gone. Instead, I found another young woman whom I persuaded to go with me to the Refuge. Sister Mildred met us at the door and greeted us warmly. She was my favourite of the All Saints Sisters, as they were called. She took the young woman by the hand and led her through to the shelter, where she would be given a bed and food and safety in return for work. She would also be taught domestic skills, and given spiritual guidance. Then, when she was ready, the Sisters would try to place her as a servant with a good family.

And so began what I called 'my work'. I walked the streets of Cape Town, finding destitute women, and offering to take them to the Refuge. It was often difficult to get out during the week, as I had to get the children up and off to school, prepare and serve breakfast to the hotel guests, and then help Lizzie with the beds and cleaning of the rooms. I seldom finished before noon, and by that time it was often too late to search for someone who had slept in the Square the night before.

And so, Sunday mornings became the time I did my work. I had continued attending Ouma's church, even after she died. On Sundays, Lizzie would make breakfast for the guests, and there was no cleaning of rooms. I then set off early, taking along with me any of the children who wanted to come – always Georgina, often Hermann, and sometimes Bertha, too.

My plan was to 'save' a woman a week. I would talk to her and hopefully drop her off at the Refuge and then go on to church, often arriving after the service had started. A Sunday seldom went by that I did not find a woman or girl to help. I warned the children not to tell their father, and we always managed to attend part of the Church service, in case Trangott asked them about it.

One Sunday I had just taken a young woman to the Refuge and was on my way to church when I saw Sophia Fisher, a friend of Auntie Dinah's daughter, walking towards me.

'Good morning, Sophia,' I greeted her. 'Do you live close by?'

Sophia looked embarrassed. 'I am staying at the Refuge,' she said.

Then she told me the story of how she had narrowly escaped death the week before. She had been walking home after a night at the Dock Road Hotel, when someone came out of a side street and accosted her from behind. She was terrified, sure that it was the Strangler, for this is what they called the man who had been raping and killing prostitutes. He started dragging her down the side street towards one of the old carriage houses. She kicked at him and he stabbed at her with a sharp object, cutting her shoulder. Just then, a carriage came down the street – a cabby on his way to collect his employer from the Dock Road Hotel. Her assailant let her go and ran off down the alley.

Fortunately, the driver of the carriage recognised Sophia from Dock Road, and helped her up into the carriage and brought her to the Refuge.

'How did you come to be doing that?' I shuddered at the idea of Sophia being a prostitute.

'My father died, and it was just me and my sister,' she explained. 'It was hard to find work. Then my sister found work in Caledon. But I didn't want to go to Caledon. I boarded with the people next door. I couldn't find work. This was the only way I could make money to pay my rent.' Sophia adjusted the *kapdoek* around her head. 'But I'm looking for work. No matter what position, or how little I earn, I'll take it. I'm not going to give the Strangler another chance.'

'Would you like a job in the hotel?' I shut off the voice in my head that said Trangott would be angry. 'We are short of someone to help in the kitchen with breakfast and dinners. You could stay on at the Refuge and work for us.'

But it was worth risking Trangott's wrath to see the gratitude on her face. 'Yes, oh yes, thank you. When can I start?'

'Today. Now.' It would be best for her to be there, already at work, when Trangott got back from meeting guests at the docks. Georgina reached out and held Sophia's hand as we walked back to the hotel.

I was right. Trangott was furious.

'I make decisions in my hotel,' he shouted at me later that night.

'Please, you will wake the children,' I warned.

'I wake everybody,' he raged. '*Gott*, woman! It is Bertha who should be working in the kitchen, not a whore.' His face was red, a thick vein in his neck pulsing.

'Don't call her that – she's a friend of my cousin.'

'A whore also,' he snarled. 'Well, keep your prostitute away from the guests. And this is Bertha's last year at school.'

Eventually Trangott became used to Sophia. She was hardworking and friendly, and the guests liked her. Later on he even allowed her to look after the front desk. She stayed with us till the end. I wonder what has happened to her now.

Naturally, I did not tell Trangott about my 'other work'. But Sophia knew, and sometimes came with me if I needed her help in persuading a woman. 'You are like a day-time Sister Nannie,' Sophia once told me. Sister Nannie was the name some of the girls gave to Mrs Pfaff. 'But Mrs Pfaff only helps European or white girls,' Sophia said, 'us coloureds she leaves for the Strangler.'

Later, when I worked with Mrs Pfaff in the Women's Christian Temperance Union, I had many arguments with her – she believed that the worst aspect of prostitution in Cape Town was that 'white women go with native or coloured men'.

Dear Maria

Today in court, Bellows produced a doctor's certificate for Sebastian's absence last week. Magistrate Van Deventer accepted it, cancelled the warrant of arrest, reinstated bail and set a date for 'further trial' for next week. I hope Sebastian won't find some other ailment next week. It seems to me that he and Mr Bellows are deliberately dragging the trial out – hoping perhaps that the witnesses will get tired of turning up.

I chatted to Nikki for a few minutes during the break for tea, and then caught the train back home. I didn't get off in Muizenberg, but decided to go through to Kalk Bay Harbour for lunch. Then I came to one of my favourite places – a bench in the little graveyard of the Holy Trinity Church in Kalk Bay.

And here, Maria, I discovered where I had seen the name Rebecca Melrose before. On a gravestone in the shadow of a gnarled milkwood tree, I read:

Rebecca Melrose

1847–1893

Beloved sister of Neville Melrose

Small fynbos shrubs outline the grave, and a birdbath surrounded by smooth round pebbles ensures that the grave is visited regularly.

She must surely have been your friend? Especially since she was born in 1847, exactly 100 years before my own birthdate. And then –

she died the same year as Trangott, and the year before you died. So many coincidences. How I wish you could tell me the story, great-grandmother. I feel as if I am wandering around the edges of your life and then I plunge – but I don't know whether it is into my own imagination or into the truth.

I imagine you and Rebecca walking together on Muizenberg beach, or watching the fishing boats coming into Kalk Bay, or sitting on the rocks at Danger Beach, and talking about the latest meeting of the Women's Christian Temperance Union.

Rebecca was nine years younger than you. If you met at the first meeting of the Women's Christian Temperance Union in July 1889, she would have been 42 and you 51. What was a friendship like between two no-longer-young women at that time? Could you get away from the hotel, from Trangott, and the children? Or did you take the children with you when you went to Kalk Bay to visit Rebecca? Georgina, your youngest, must have been about ten at the time. What did you and Rebecca talk about? What was she like?

I imagine her as a tall, slim woman. A fine, intelligent face with dark eyes – her black hair wild, unruly.

I see her waiting on the Kalk Bay platform to meet your train. A steam train, of course, the engine puffing smoke into the sea air as it chugs its way alongside the ocean from Muizenberg. It is a Wednesday afternoon in April – a perfect autumn day. The train hoots as it pulls into Kalk Bay station.

I see you appear at the open door of an end carriage, and as the train stops, you get off, holding a young girl with one hand and a picnic basket with the other. Somehow, you also manage to hold a parasol.

You look around, a little anxiously, then your face lights up as you see Rebecca move lithely towards you, dressed in what looks like multiple layers of brightly coloured cloth. Her skirts billow as she passes people on the platform. She takes no notice of their stares. Her wide smile stretches across her face as she hurries towards you. Georgina drops your hand and runs towards her..Rebecca scoops the child up and hugs her, and then embraces you, knocking your smart hat off your head. Laughing, the three of you chase it as it spins along the platform. For a brief moment, you burst into radiance.

circle five

CROSSING BORDERS

*Writing is not arriving; most of the time it's not arriving.
One has to go away, leave the self. How far must one not
arrive in order to write? One must walk as far as the night.
One's own night. Walking through the self toward the dark.*

—Helen Cixous, *Three Steps on the Ladder of Writing*

Valkenberg Asylum,
Tuesday 24 June 1894

In the cold, cruel daylight, we are reduced to the idiotic, the
pathetic, the filthy, and the helpless. Only at night, when the
darkness brings a luminosity to our dreams and memories,
can we return to the tragic, the violent, the passionate, the
terrified selves that brought us to this place.

Is dying like dreaming, I wonder – being transported to a
strange yet familiar place without effort or pain of transition?
Like birth, it is surely a mysterious process that takes its own
course.

I feel I have experienced two births. My second birth began
when I read the strange story of Lyndall in *The Story of an
African Farm* – a novel written by Olive Schreiner, a woman
whose ideas disturbed our somnolent society. I had hoped for
an awakening on marrying Trangott. My life with Father, with
its predicable routine and its drudgery, had left me dulled and
only half awake. But Trangott, like the prince in *Sleeping
Beauty*, fell in love with a sleeping woman. As I began to
awaken, Trangott felt the first pangs of betrayal.

I remember, so clearly, the day I saw Schreiner's novel in
Juta's Bookshop window. I was on my way to Mrs Kramer's
Drapery to buy material to make new curtains for the hotel
lounge. I went into Juta's, picked up a copy, opened it and
read the first paragraph:

*The full African moon poured down its light from the
blue sky into the wide, lonely plain. The dry, sandy
earth, with its coating of stunted 'karoo' bushes a few
inches high, the low hills that skirted the plain, the milk-
bushes with their long, finger-like leaves, all were
touched by a weird and an almost oppressive beauty as
they lay in the white light.*

I felt strangely mesmerised by the book – as if I, too, had
been 'touched by a weird beauty'. Using two shillings from
the curtain money, I bought it. It had been published a few
years before under the nom de plume of Ralph Irons, but the
volume in my hands was a new edition, with Olive Schreiner's
name on the cover. Right from the time I'd first heard about
Miss Schreiner, some years before, I was drawn to this
remarkable woman. Like me, she was born and grew up in
the Cape Colony. Although she was only 28 when the book
was published, her writing revealed a deep understanding of
the predicament of women. She said, 'When I was a child and
a young girl in my teens, the thing that absorbed my thoughts
and feelings was the position of women. A terrible, burning
bitterness was in my heart about it.'

How well I knew that 'terrible burning bitterness'.

I did not go to Mrs Kramer's Drapery that day, but went
home instead, and started reading. When Trangott came in,
hours later, he found me with the book in my hands. His
anger seemed out of proportion at the time, but looking back,

perhaps he sensed that this was the crack in the shell of my second hatching, and that he would soon be unable to stop my inevitable emergence.

Trangott blamed the book and its influence for my involvement in the Women's Christian Temperance Union. I was 'neglecting the children for this women's nonsense', he said. Ironically, one of the first issues the Union addressed was very important for children – all children, including our own. The Union was at the time working to change the law on the age of consent. I recall Mrs Brown, our President, making an urgent speech at one of our meetings, saying, 'This law touches the very core of our womanhood and should stir every fibre of our body with shame and indignation.' My Georgina was nine at the time, and many of the other women also had young daughters. We wanted the age of consent to be raised from ten to eighteen, though some were prepared to compromise, and consider sixteen. We had a personal stake in this law – all around us was evidence of vulnerable, violated young women.

'Will you be taking new members? If so, I should like to join you.'

A rich, textured voice interrupted our meeting one Saturday afternoon late in 1889. We had been working on a report for our newsletter, *The White Ribbon*.

Looking up, I saw what seemed to be an apparition – a woman wearing multicoloured skirts and men's lace-up boots, her thick black curls unrestrained by ribbons or a bonnet. The woman's bare hands rested on her hips, and she had neither a parasol nor a shawl. She stood, legs apart, as if she had just got off a horse. Which she had, I later learned.

Clearing her throat to disguise the surprise we all felt, Mrs Evans, our chairwoman, said politely, 'Good afternoon ... Miss ... Mrs ...?'

'Rebecca, Rebecca Melrose, from Kalk Bay,' and she strode up to our table, offering her hand to Mrs Evans.

'Well, my dear Miss Melrose, you are welcome to attend our next monthly meeting, and to sign up with our President. Here today, we are having a sub-committee meeting, but you are welcome to join us – if you like – having come all the way from Kalk Bay.' She sounded uncertain. Rebecca accepted immediately and shook our hands vigorously as Mrs Evans introduced us all.

This was my introduction to Rebecca Melrose – who strode into my life and overturned it the moment she entered that room. We continued the meeting while Rebecca merely observed, and listened, saying very little. 'I had to make sure it wasn't going to be another ladies' tea party,' she confided wryly some time later.

The *White Ribbon* report covered our Lock Hospital campaign. Our plan was to challenge the Contagious Diseases Act, in terms of which women could be incarcerated for compulsory testing and treatment. Even after release they were listed on a register and subject to regular visits from the inspectors. We were outraged that the law protected men and penalised women. Rebecca Melrose listened quietly as we discussed the matter, and left with details of the date and time of our next general meeting – which was to be held, as usual, in the Sea Point Town Hall.

When I arrived at the Town Hall the following week, I looked around for Rebecca. When I did not see her, I decided she had changed her mind. Then, just as the meeting was drawing to a close, I saw her standing against the wall at the back. People had started to leave, but she didn't move. She seemed to be waiting for me. When I approached her, she smiled broadly and walked towards me, her hand outstretched.

'How nice to see you again, Maria,' she said. 'I've joined the Union and hope to be allocated to your sub-committee. You are, I believe, working on legislation?'

'Oh, yes. Yes, that's nice.' She seemed afire with energy – and I could not help feeling dull and matronly in contrast.

'I also signed up for the Franchise Committee. The only way we can bring about change, real change, is if we have the vote.'

'I agree,' I said weakly, 'I am also a member of that sub-committee.'

'Wonderful,' she said, 'so we'll see each other often. Shall we have tea together, and you can bring me up to date on the work?'

I ignored the voice in my head that would have me answer, 'Another time, thanks, Miss Melrose, I have to get back to the hotel, to my family.' Instead, I suggested we go to the Upstairs Ladies' Room at the Café Royal. I would tell Trangott that the meeting had gone on till late, and that I had had to wait for the omnibus.

Rebecca and I spoke for more than two hours, talking about our lives and our ideas, and finding that we agreed on many things – including our views on Olive Schreiner's novel. Rebecca had recently met Miss Schreiner when she and her brother, Neville, were invited to dinner with Will Schreiner, at his house near the Company Gardens. Miss Schreiner was also there, having travelled from Matjiesfontein in the Karoo hinterland. She and Rebecca found that they had much in common, and started up a correspondence.

'Not without arguments and disagreements,' Rebecca told me. 'Miss Schreiner has strong views on most subjects and she argues them fiercely and fearlessly.'

'Not unlike you,' I thought to myself, deciding that Miss Melrose and Miss Schreiner had probably met their match in each other.

'She lives in Matjiesfontein, for health reasons, but also to have solitude for her writing.' Rebecca explained, 'And I understand that – the need to live in such a way that permits a creative existence.'

She went on to tell me how she, Rebecca, was born and grew up in Kanaladorp, as District Six was called at the time. Her father was a musician and string-instrument maker, her mother a seamstress and bonnet maker. Both

Rebecca and Neville learned to play music while young.

'Neville choose the violin, and I loved the sound and feel of the cello,' Rebecca said. 'He was very talented, but studied law when he left school, to please our mother. And I ended up as a music teacher, teaching cello and piano at the Good Hope Seminary.'

'Although he qualified as an attorney, Neville's real passion is writing,' she went on to explain. 'He writes wonderful adventure stories for children. And I always wanted to be an artist – a painter. When our parents died, within a month of each other, we decided to start a business together. We bought an old dilapidated coach house in Kalk Bay, renovated it to include a few guest rooms, acquired new coaches and horses, and in this way we started our weekend coach trips.'

On Saturday mornings, Rebecca and Neville would collect their hotel guests from Cape Town or Wynberg Station and transport them by carriage to Melrose House, where they would have lunch and then spend the afternoon on Muizenberg beach, or go for a drive to Simonstown. The guests returned by carriage after lunch on Sunday, well-rested and entertained.

'Neville sees to the kitchen, and I drive the carriages,' Rebecca informed me, amused at my surprise. 'This arrangement keeps us busy on weekends, but our weekdays are relatively free – for Neville to write, and for me to paint.'

So it happened that my friendship with Rebecca was the final crack in my shell, enabling me to emerge into the world, somewhat tentatively, but determined not to retreat into my previous suffocating existence. She seemed to open windows in my soul, teaching me to take in the fresh sea air, to fill my lungs with it, and to soar with the gulls.

How far I am from soaring now.

Lesson Five – Crossing Borders

Writing brings us to the frontier of the forbidden and helps us to trespass it. It is about going beyond, about breaking through the known, the human, and advancing in the direction of the terrifying, of our own end ... there where the other begins.

Heléne Cixous, *Three Steps on the Ladder of Writing.*

Writing at the edge of ourselves is to cross boundaries – to cross borders in ourselves, and in our writing. To do this, we must write further-than-ourselves, and so discover what Cixous calls 'our poetic genius'.

Writing should be like dreaming. In dreams we speak to the dead, make love with a stranger, leave someone to die, drive over a cliff. We can be violent, selfish, lustful, murderous – as well as heroic, passionate and tender. So, too, in writing. Writing at the periphery of ourselves is writing that makes us tremble as we cross the threshold.

Writing that stays within boundaries is 'careful' writing. It is writing with little energy. To write 'well', we must write with innocence and abandon, surpassing ourselves. We must write like a child learning to walk, who 'rushes, faster than herself, as if the secret of walking were ahead of her.' (Cixous)

Writing further-than-ourselves requires courage, and love. It is writing that is always beyond us, writing into the darkness, on the inside of oneself, away from the comfort and confines of organized thought.

- *Describe your own thresholds and borders – in yourself and in your writing.*
- *Write about a moment, in your own or in someone else's life, when you crossed a border or stepped over a threshold.*

Anna Bertrand,

Cape Town, 2004

Dear Maria

I am sitting in a coffee shop overlooking the little fishing harbour in
Kalk Bay, trying to do my writing exercises from the Workbook. The
waiter brings me a cappuccino without my asking. I am a 'regular'
here, and come whenever I need an injection of noise, activity and
good coffee.

I feel stuck, without imagination or energy. I can't seem to make
the leap the author talks about – the leap into the dark, the unknown.
The contradiction between the confused, clumsy self that I am
writing about, and the self that I need to be to write about it
properly, overwhelms me. I try to extend my reach in writing, to write
bigger and better than I am. I strain to see to the end of my vision
where things get fuzzy and blurred. I need to stretch from the
shoulder, to lean further than is safe and reach my open hand
towards the bigger, larger possibility of myself. To touch with
trembling fingertips, knowing I might lean too far, and fall.

I think I am always reaching into the unknown, afraid to touch it,
yet reaching anyway. Do we all do that? Did you, Maria? In my writing,
I reach for my future self, for the woman who is bigger, more
complete, richer than my 'now' self. But when the words are written
here, on a page in this crumpled notebook, they stare at me, accusing
me of cowardice, of pretending to reach – but not all the way, not
beyond the boundaries, not to the furthest wave in the ocean. It's like
trying to do sign language without fingers, just square clumsy stumps,
fists, waving in the air. Perhaps I can break through in poetry ...

I try to write further-than-myself
beyond the literal
to the edge in me,
I try to walk through
the red-light district of myself,
taste the decadent in me,
touch the sad, the wounded,
the desolate and the crazed,
walk through the nightmarish place
where nothing makes sense,
smell the bag lady in me,
the prostitute, the dope-addict,
the sodden drunk in a sleazy bar
in me.

I try to reach the jagged edge
that cuts through the cardboard
of my everyday life,
pulls at the padding that muffles
the ache of the world
in me.

And I find – I am afraid.

Afraid to find the emptiness
of a small town backyard
in me,
the chipped concrete floor
dusty junk and broken glass
in me,
Afraid to find the stray cat
scrounging for leftovers
in the dead of a shabby night
in me.

I feel the edge of it, and am afraid.

'Johanna, my maidservant, is in Lock Hospital. We must try to get her released, she is not a prostitute!' Mary Johnson, a new member, faced us one Tuesday afternoon as we sat in a meeting of the Legislation committee of the Women's Union.

'Two inspectors came to our house yesterday, looking for servant girls in the neighbourhood who were working as prostitutes at the docks at night. They kept questioning Johanna until she signed the paper they brought. She told me she signed, thinking it would make them go away. But it was an admission that she was a prostitute, and they took her off to Lock Hospital. I was able to visit this morning, but they would not release her until the tests are completed. The poor child is only seventeen!'

'Even if they do release her, she will be on the Register of Prostitutes,' another member observed. 'So they can arrest her at any time and take her back.'

'Neville, my brother, is a lawyer,' Rebecca interrupted. 'I will ask him if we can bring a case against the Lock, or the inspectors. He no longer practises as an attorney, but he is still registered and is very sympathetic to our work. I'll go back to Kalk Bay and ask him immediately,' Rebecca jumped up. 'Will you come with me, Maria?'

I declined. It was a two-hour carriage trip to Kalk Bay, and I had to get back to the hotel and the children.

'There will be another time,' Rebecca said. 'Would you like to come out over the weekend? We have no guests this Sunday. Bring your children with you. I will send a carriage for you on Sunday morning.'

Trangott insisted on making a family outing of the Sunday trip to Kalk Bay. 'We have not done this for a long time,' he said, 'Sophia can prepare lunch for the guests.'

Rebecca and Neville welcomed us at the door as the carriage pulled up and we all got out. 'I don't know if you expected so many of us,' I half-apologised to Rebecca. 'No one wanted to be left out.'

'You are all most welcome,' said Neville, shaking Trangott's hand, then mine and each of the children's in turn. Georgina took his hand solemnly and looked shyly into his kind eyes.

Leaving Neville talking to Trangott, Rebecca took the rest of us on a tour of the house – a large three-storey, white-washed house with a coach house attached, and stables behind for the horses. Rebecca and Neville lived on the ground floor, the two guest rooms were upstairs, and the airy attic was filled with Rebecca's bold, colourful canvasses.

'I'm a painter,' she told the children as we filed into her studio, and she showed us her paintings – of fishing boats, and portraits of local Kalk Bay fisherfolk, all in vibrant splashes of colour, and alive with movement.

The day was windless, the air mild. Neville had packed lunch and we set off to the fishing cove. Rebecca spread rugs on the beach and we all gathered around the picnic basket.

When we had eaten the last crumb of the delicious ham sandwiches, and we'd each had a large slice of Neville's apple pie, Rebecca took my hand. 'Come, Maria, we have some Women's Union business to discuss,' and she pulled me up. 'We are going for a walk,' she announced to the others. And so, arm in arm, we wandered over to the rocks at the end of the beach, talking at first, and then falling silent as we watched the waves crashing onto the rocks. The waves seemed to echo the pounding in my chest. I am happy, I realised with some surprise.

Suddenly, inexplicably, I felt a swell of sadness. I turned my face to the wind, not wanting Rebecca to see my tears. If she did notice them, she simply squeezed my arm, saying nothing.

I looked back at the others. Trangott was making sandcastles with the older children, and Georgina sat close to Neville, deep in conversation. Rebecca and I walked slowly back towards the group of people on the beach who seemed at once so close and so far from us.

Anna Bertrand,

Cape Town, 2004

Dear Maria

Ralph Sebastian's trial started today with both Mr Bellows, his lawyer, and Sebastian present. The police gave evidence, Mr Bellows trying unsuccessfully to throw doubt on aspects of their investigation. It looks to me as if Nikki is building a solid case against Sebastian. And Sebastian himself is not looking too happy.

Nikki called her main witness – Judith, a sex-worker – who had been with Sebastian and Isobel the day Isobel was killed. Today, to impress the Magistrate, Judith wore sensible shoes and a carefully pressed off-the-peg slack-suit, and looked like a school-librarian. She told the court how Sebastian had offered her and Isobel a drink in the bar of the Burgundy Hotel in Main Road. How Sebastian had bought a bottle of brandy from the bar and suggested they all go down to the beach and 'have a party'.

'Had you met the accused before that day?' Nikki asked.

'Yes, he's always at the bar. He usually went for Isobel, but she wouldn't go with him any more.'

'Why? Did she tell you?'

'She said she was scared of him. She told me he had once tried to hurt her and she didn't want to go alone with him again. That's why I said I would go with them to the beach.'

'So the three of you went down to Queen's beach?'

'Yes, he ...' pointing to Sebastian, 'he said he would give us a lot of money. He showed us the notes in his wallet.'

'What happened when you got to the beach?'

'We sat on the bench in the parking area. Drinking the brandy. Then he asked Isobel to go down to the beach with him where the toilets are.'

'Did she?'

'She said no, and went to stand against the railings.'

'What happened then?'

'He went over to her and tried to pull her towards the steps down to the beach. She pushed him away and swore at him. He grabbed her and she was struggling with him.'

'And then?'

'I started to go to help her. He had pushed her backwards against the railing. When he saw me coming, he asked me if he should throw her over.'

'What did you say?'

'I shouted at him, No, let her go! But then he lifted her up and pushed her over.'

Judith was crying now.

'What did the accused do then?'

'He laughed. He just laughed and walked away from the railing.'

'What did you do?'

'He was coming towards me now. I was scared, so I turned around and started running.'

'Did he follow you?'

'No. I ran all the way to the Sea Point Police Station and told the police what had happened. They drove me back to the parking lot, and there he was, just sitting on the bench like nothing had happened! She blew her nose and stared defiantly at Sebastian.

Nikki thanked Judith. By then it was nearly the end of the day, and Magistrate Van Deventer adjourned the court till Monday.

After congratulating Nikki on doing a fine job, I came here, to put in an hour at Manuscripts and Archives before closing time. I was interested in finding out about attitudes towards prostitution in your day, Maria. And in the minutes of the meetings of the Women's Christian Temperance Union, I was amazed at the progressive attitudes, and concern for prostitutes, they expressed. A resolution adopted at one of its first meetings, reads:

> As a Union, our hearts burn within us at the indignity done to
> women through the Contagious Diseases Act, and we pledge
> ourselves to use our influence to bring about its repeal
> (WCTU executive Minutes, 1889).

With the passing of the Act had come the building of the Lock Hospital in Roeland Street, where women were literally locked up while undergoing testing for sexually transmitted diseases. The Act made it legal for police and specially-appointed inspectors to arrest any female suspects and take them to Lock Hospital for compulsory testing. If found to have traces of syphilis or gonorrhoea, they were confined to the hospital until the weekly test showed no further traces. After this, they were entered on a Register of Prostitutes.

Doctors from England who supported the Contagious Diseases Act in their own country, were recruited to the Cape Town Lock Hospital. The minutes show that one of the first doctors to arrive was Dr Feather, who had been working at the similarly named Lock Hospital in London.

Dr Feather. Was he any relation to Dorothy Feather, the woman who was with you at Valkenberg, Maria? You would probably have come across him in your attempt to get the Contagious Diseases Act repealed. It would not have been easy, with the kind of attitudes from law-makers and authorities that I came across in this statement by the Attorney General, T L Graham:

> *From what I have gathered from clergymen and others who are constantly coming into contact with kafirs and natives generally, it appears that a considerable traffic is being carried on in Cape Town between aboriginal natives and white European women. There are certain houses in Cape Town which any kafir could frequent, and as long as he was able to pay the sum demanded, he could have illicit intercourse with these white European women. This is a matter of the gravest importance, for once the barriers are broken down between the European and native races in this country there is no limit to the terrible dangers to which women will be submitted, particularly in isolated places.*
> — Attorney General, T L Graham, House of Assembly Debate. (1892)

Rebecca joined the Women's Christian Temperance Union
because she said there was no other organisation to join, apart
from the *Vrouesendingbond* – which was an Afrikaans women's
organisation and far more conventional in many of its
attitudes than the Women's Union.

At the Women's Union meetings, Rebecca seemed to take a
sly pleasure in shocking the more conservative members. I
remember a meeting one afternoon in the Central Methodist
Church Hall. Mrs Pfaff had just welcomed everyone when
Rebecca arrived, her black hair tumbling about her face, her
multicoloured dress spattered with paint. Later, over tea, she
told me she had been working on a portrait, and had lost
track of the time, so she had taken a carriage without
changing her clothes.

Rebecca caused consternation at that meeting by
announcing that she could not call herself a Christian. Her
mother was Jewish, but she refused to give that as a reason for
not being a Christian.

'I cannot conform to any religion which restricts women,'
Rebecca explained later when we met at the Café Royal. 'It is
one of the things that Olive Schreiner and I have been
discussing in our letters.'

On another occasion, during a meeting on plans to
eliminate prostitution, Rebecca announced to the Union, 'I

have many friends who are prostitutes. And I often go to visit them at night, in the taverns and the Dock Road Hotel.'

I doubt that many of the women in the room believed her, but what she said was true. What Rebecca did not tell them, though, was that she very often went dressed as a man.

'If James Barry could get away with it, so can I,' she told me. 'Anyway, it protects me from the men who frequent those places.'

Rebecca admired the ambitious and daring Dr James Barry, respected Inspector General of Hospitals in the Cape Colony who was appointed to the position after 46 years in the British Army. How shocked polite Cape society was when Dr Barry's secret was revealed, and 'he' was found to be a woman after her death in 1865.

Rebecca was intrigued and excited at the idea of wearing men's clothes – at the freedom this gave a woman in a world that belonged to men. She told me about the time she and Neville had gone to the Admiral's Fancy Dress Ball in Simonstown. Rebecca chose to wear military uniform, and scandalised the company at large, and the Admiral's wife in particular, by requesting a dance with her.

Dear Maria

'More coffee?', I imagine I hear you say one evening after dinner at the Germania. Your mind is elsewhere. The guests sense this and look reproachful. They are paying, not only for their rooms and food, but also to be the focus of their host's attention – for you to indulge and fuss about them in a way their own mothers probably never did.

Trangott also seems distracted this evening. His enjoyment in being the sociable hotel keeper has seemed rather forced recently. And his mood lies heavily on you. It seems that Trangott, too, relies for his *bonhomie* on your active involvement in the life of the hotel.

You aren't really aware of this, of course – in fact, you would probably be surprised if you were to be told that all these people's well-being depended on you. And you couldn't know that in your absence, the hotel was bleak and gloomy, and everyone – from the guests to your children and Trangott – felt abandoned, which made them sullen.

I've been at the South African Library all morning, looking for clues about Trangott's death in old copies of the *Cape Times* and *Cape Argus*. Nothing, so far. My eyes are tired, and so I have taken my lunch from the locker and come here, to the Gardens, to clear my head. I am sitting on a bench under a magnificent wild fig tree, so huge it must certainly have been here in your time.

The air is cold, but still. The gulls appear from nowhere as soon as I take my sandwich from the lunch box. Small and perky, they stand on their straight little legs, looking round-eyed at me, their beaks eager, waiting to be thrown some crusts. A squirrel runs in a straight line down a tree trunk, then hovers at the bottom, its tail quivering, its front paws ready to snatch a crust before the gulls get it.

As I sit here, Maria, I seem to hear you calling. It is a deep sound, like a whale calling across the ocean, reverberating in my body, calling me into the darkness of my own night. Calling me to the edge of myself. I tremble, afraid to cross the border, afraid of casting doubt on my identity, afraid to find you no longer in the margins of my life, but instead to find that I exist in the margins of your life.

Yet I yearn for the silence that is you. I yearn to transform that silence into words. I long for the release that this will bring. Fearfully, I take the step over the threshold into the night that is you, looking for a chink of light in the darkness that will break through into your heart, your life. And then I find myself here, sitting on a bench under a wild fig in the Company Gardens, and I imagine arranging long, full skirts, folding a parasol, and waiting for Rebecca to appear.

I see her coming along the path, wearing a brilliant green skirt and matching waistcoat, but carrying neither a parasol, nor a hat, nor gloves, her hair blowing freely in the wind. I feel your spirit lift, a rush of heat reddening your cheeks as she stands, smiling, in front of you.

'Sorry I'm late, Maria.' Still, she stands there.

You say nothing, as you absorb her life and colour.

'Fine ... fine,' you manage. 'Sit here,' and you gesture to a place next to you on the bench.

'Did you have difficulty leaving the hotel?'

'No, Trangott thinks I've gone to the bootmaker.'

'How long do we have until you must go back?' She takes your hand and you feel the heat in your cheeks again.

'Half an hour, perhaps.'

'As always, not long enough.' She strokes your hand. You wonder if she will kiss you goodbye again today, as she did the last time you met here. She did it so lightly, as if it were such an ordinary thing for two friends to do, but it wasn't on your cheek as usual, and the feel of her lips on yours stayed with you long afterwards.

She is looking quietly at you. You hold her look, breathless. Her mouth comes closer, and then, again, her lips touch yours. You pray that she won't draw back, and you press your lips timidly against hers. But she does draw back.

'We should probably not meet like this here,' she says softly, your hand in both of hers.

'Where, then?' You are surprised at your own boldness.

'We'll find a place.' She touches a button on your bodice, her hand lightly lingering, your breast melting beneath her touch.

You nod helplessly. A mother and her small boy appear along the path, and Rebecca's hand drops to her side. You try to settle your face into an expression that feels normal. The mother and child pass by.

'Are you happy, Maria?' she gently asks. You nod again, trying to find your voice.

'What will we do?' you ask.

Rebecca gives a confident wave of her hand, dismissing your doubt and confusion.

circle six

PATTERNS AND SHAPES

In writing of experience, we discover what it was,
and in the writing create the pattern we seem to have lived.

—Carolyn G Heilbrun, *The Education of a Woman*

Anna Bertrand,

Cape Town, 2004

Dear Maria

I have just found mention in Dorothy's file of her sister, Hester. Right near the back I came across a letter to Dr Dodds from the Secretary of the Colonial Orphan Chamber and Trust Company, which administered the money left by James Feather in his will to his daughters. It reads:

24 January 1906

Dear Dr Dodds
I have yours of the 22 inst. I do not think it prudent to remove Miss Hester from Grahamstown Asylum where she appears to be quite comfortable and happy, and we do not know whether the two sisters may get on together. It may destroy the comfort and happiness of both. I therefore think it best to leave well alone.

Yours faithfully
G T H Eliot
Secretary

That was 1906. Dorothy would have been in Valkenberg for fifteen years by then. And Hester was obviously sent to the Grahamstown Asylum. Why were they were separated in the first place? According to his death certificate, James Feather died in 1903 at the age of 72 – so this discussion as to whether to allow the two sisters to be together arose three years after his death.

I can hardly believe that they were 'comfortable and happy', in any case. The pages of handwritten entries in Dorothy's record, stretching over the 53 years that she was in Valkenberg Asylum, tell their own story.

On 30 April 1892 – a year after she was admitted – the record reads: *Full of imaginary ailments. Delusions of persecution. Wants to die.*

Two years later, on 19 July 1894, it states: *Is obviously hallucinating and discourses with unseen people. As when she was first admitted, she expresses Foolish Delusions, one of which is that her father raped her.*

On 8 October 1905, when Dorothy was 47 and had been in Valkenberg for fourteen years, the entry reads: *She is deteriorating mentally. She talks and mumbles to herself. Smiles foolishly, is restless, unoccupied.*

In 1914, the notes state: *No mental change to record. Sits in one position all day, grabbing her overall with both hands. Time passes lightly over this profoundly demented woman. She looks no more than 40, though her present age is 56.*

Ten years later, on 12 April 1924, when she was 66, the observation notes report: *Sits in a constrained attitude, pulling her skirt tightly across her lap. She looks up quickly in answer to questions and smiles inanely. She is retarded, profoundly disorientated for time and place, but she knew today was Wednesday and that she had sausage and egg for breakfast. She remains motionless for hours on end.*

In July 1926, when she was 68, the notes state: *Sits about all day* in a fixed attitude and takes no notice of her surroundings. Circulation is sluggish. *Skin on back of hands becoming very discoloured, shiny and atrophied owing to the clenched attitude in which she holds them. Seems to have no idea of time and place.*

In 1929, when she was 71: *No change in her mannerisms. Smiles broadly, shuts her eyes and clutches her dress with both hands.*

Two years later, at 73: *This feeble dement is only interested when food is mentioned and will say 'Yes, please,' if asked if she wants custard, but usually her remarks are irrelevant.*

In April 1933: *Deteriorated and demented. Fidgets about aimlessly and restlessly. Wet and dirty.*

Nearly a year later, in February 1934, she was transferred to Ward F and described thus: *Stupid, asocial and indifferent. Her speech is thick and indistinct. She gives little information. Her habits are dirty and she abuses herself. Her demeanour is foolish. She is at times cheeky and impatient. She refuses to occupy herself. Her conversation is rambling and incoherent.*

In 1937, the records state: *This helpless aged dement leads a vegetative existence. Her only interest being food, but she can no longer converse relevantly even on that subject.*

In 1939, when she was 81, they described her as follows: *This old lady is deteriorated mentally and physically. No information can be obtained from her. She has swelling of the feet due to cardiac failure.*

A year later: *Dull, demented, faulty habits, helpless.*

In 1942, at the age of 84: *There has been a further deterioration in the mental condition of this patient. She is completely demented and is quite incapable of supplying any information at all. Physically she is quite helpless and has to be assisted in every respect by the nursing staff. She requires to be dressed, washed, and fed. Her intimate habits are faulty.*

Did 'faulty' habits mean not being able to keep herself clean or go to the toilet when she needed to – or did it imply something worse? Most records of the patients, especially on admission, mention 'faulty' habits. Were you accused of faulty habits, Maria? Was your involvement in the WCTU and trying to get the vote for women considered a 'faulty' habit? And what about your relationship with Rebecca?

The ward is restless, haunted by the moonlight draping its bluish tinge over our beds and hollowing out our minds. I watch the sway of the trees outside the window, their winter branches silhouetted against the indigo sky. Dorothy thrashes about in her bed, her jumbled words urgent and desperate. The footsteps of the night nurse clatter as she comes down the corridor, and the light from her candle distorting the features of her face as she stands a moment in the doorway. She enters, sets down her candle on the table next to Dorothy's bed, and attempts to soothe her.

Shadows flicker on the wall behind the bed, like the shadows in the candlelight of my memory. The shadows of women who walked at night in fear. Shadows of children afraid of their fathers. Shadows of women working, always working. I see women like Ouma carrying heavy loads of washing, servant girls in cold houses, toiling from four in the morning till late at night – and still not enough money to buy a new pair of shoes. I see Emily Booth, hopeful, bags in hand, anticipating her new life. And I see her keenness and music, together with her innocence, discarded just like her limp body. And I see my children – a dark shadow in each of their hearts that no lamp can disperse.

And Dorothy? What of the shadow she carries in her heart? Since I have been here, she has had no visitors at all. If her father is still telling the story that she returned to England, there is no one who knows she is here. James Feather will certainly not visit her. I imagine him sitting at this moment in the armchair in the lounge of the Germania Hotel, boasting about his luck at the gambling table and enjoying the cigars and whisky provided by the new hotel owner. And, in all likelihood, he is still conducting tests on prostitutes at the Lock Hospital.

The Union received many negative reports about the treatment of women at the hospital. I was charged with approaching Dr Feather about this. I took the opportunity to confront him one evening. He was alone in the lounge of the Germania, sitting, as usual, in the armchair by the fire, waiting for his whisky.

'Dr Feather ...' I handed him a glass. 'I would like to ask you about the treatment procedures at the Lock Hospital.'

He glared up at me. 'Yes? What about them?'

'The Women's Union has received complaints about the rough treatment many of the women experience.'

'Oh yes? Which whore complained?' His tone was sarcastic.

'Oh, no. Not anyone in particular, and not someone undergoing treatment at the moment,' I hastened to tell him. 'It is a general complaint. They say the examination is very painful.'

I did not tell him that he had been mentioned by name as one of the doctors who seemed to be deliberately rough with his examination.

'They say the instruments hurt,' I went on.

'Well, it should hurt. Make them think twice next time they try to spread their filth among decent people.' He took a large gulp from his glass and rudely turned away.

I stood there, uncertain of how best to continue. I seemed to be making matters worse.

'Anyway, why should you care?' Barely glancing up, he drained his glass. 'A decent married woman like you, a white woman, too. You surely have better things to do than keep company with kaffir bitches and bastard Hottentots.'

Impatiently, he pushed himself up from the armchair. 'What do you say about it, Trangott?' He called across to Trangott who had just come into the lounge. 'Why do you allow your wife to become involved with this nonsense?'

'Trangott has no reason to complain,' I said quickly, more to Trangott than James Feather. 'I work hard in the hotel, and take good care of my children.'

Then, in an attempt to divert James Feather off the subject. 'I hope your daughters are settled in England?'

'Pathetic creatures. But I am glad they are out of the way so you can't recruit them to your interfering women's club.' Abruptly, he made for the door.

I have no doubt he was on his way to the Dock Road Hotel. Sophia had told me he was a regular visitor while she was there. But she had never seen him with any of the women – his habit was to join the men in the noisy, smoke-filled lounge before leaving late at night.

Lesson Six – Patterns and Shapes

*The autobiographical act is an interpretation
of life that invests the past and the self with coherence
and meaning that may not have been evident
before the act of writing itself.*
—AnaLouise Keating, *Women Reading, Women Writing*

Generally, life doesn't make a very good story. It is the
connections we make, the relationship between events, and
the meanings we discover in these experiences which give
our stories shape.

Each story has a pattern that organizes random events
or experiences. It develops from small moments and
insights that cluster together. These become coherent
through the workings of the imagination, which reveals
the relationships, links and connections. The nature of
these relationships becomes clear in the process of telling
the story. So it is best if we can get out of our own way,
and allow the randomness to disappear as a mysterious
shaping power makes itself known through the form of
the story.

This means that to give our stories shape, we need to
look for the patterns, the threads that run through them.
And we discover these patterns and threads in our lives
through the process of writing. It is in telling the stories of
our lives, that we reveal the patterns we have lived.

- *Try to trace the patterns that have recurred throughout
  your life, and write about them.*
- *Think specifically about the relationships in your life
  and, as you write about them, try to identify patterns.*

Anna Bertrand,

Cape Town, 2004

Dear Maria

Writing about my life has been like digging through a layer of hard crust. I plunge with the blunt edge of my memory, feeling it clang on the hard surface. As I keep digging and scraping, excavating my hidden self, I break through in places, into the moist soil, and reach the fertile compost of my life. I am surprised at the heat under the crust, the teeming, steaming life below, as I uncover the fragments.

Are there patterns in these fragments, repetitive rhythms that have shaped me? As I listen to the melody of myself, I hear a mournful sound. I realise I am always drawn to people who elude me. Am I in search of a lost self?

I felt my first great passion at the age of twelve. The object of my longing was an aunt who used to visit from Italy once a year and stayed with my grandparents. Elegant, dark-eyed and foreign, Aunt Francesca had a way of making words sound different, and she had a laugh like a water fountain. My uncle had met her when he was posted in Italy during the war, and he stayed on and married her. They lived in Milan and came to Johannesburg at Christmas.

I remember, that Christmas in 1960, following her about every day. With her, I felt like a kite – she, the strong gust of wind that lifted me skywards. I exulted in her life-force, my string taut, my paper tail thrilling out behind.

I remember the tip of her finger on my cheek as she called me 'cara'. The day she left, I discovered how hard you fall when the wind drops. I lay on the floor of my grandparents' lounge the entire afternoon, feeling suddenly much older, and listening over and over to the 78 rpm record of Italian folk songs she had given me. As the room darkened at the end of the day, my grandfather turned the record player off and gently wrapped a rug around me. Did he somehow know that this was my first heartbreak?

Throughout my high school years I yearned to be with the bright and shiny girls, the sky-blue girls in class. My creased and grubby self longed to be like them, with clean fingernails, glossy hair, pens that didn't leak, stockings that didn't ladder, books covered in brown paper with neat edges and pictures stuck straight on the front, handwriting that stayed in the lines. I longed to be as clean and responsible as a hymn book monitor.

Later, I seemed to fall in love with women with dry karoo veld in their hearts. Women with dark and desiccated interior landscapes, impenetrable, brittle.

I find myself now, as I was that lonely afternoon as a twelve-year-old, crashed again, after my most recent and perhaps most exhilarating flight. My yearning kite string pulled once again at my centre, my head swirled with the roaring inside. I was buffeted when I saw a bruise on her neck and imagined my lips touching it, or when I breathed in the smell of perfume and cigarette smoke in her bedroom. But I was left, at last, motionless on the ground, my heart curling like a dead leaf.

                beneath
the melody
lightly
keeping company
                beneath
the musical phrases and
familiar regularity
                        the soft rain falls

                beneath
the threading sounds
treading paths of
mutual liking
                around
the edge of the tea pot
the milk jug
the sugar bowl
                a vibrato string tells
                of what might have been

                beneath
the woodwind call
charming with melody
                while feet dabble
                at the edge of a river
gently she opens the gate
and comes in
dressed in green
                        metaphors of friendship
                        deceptively simple

                beneath
the movement of eyes
and fear of approaching
                a bruise
                a soft mouth

night dreams
entwine
    and the rain falls
soaking
    the everyday skin
filling
    dry places spread wide
pouring
    through early morning windows
sinking
    into moist places
    tongue buried deep
heaven opening
    as the rain falls

Later that night, after the kiss under the wild fig in the
Company Gardens, I fought to compose my face, to calm my
movements as I sat trying to do my needlework, as usual, in the
lounge at the Germania, while Trangott saw to the guests. It
was as if I had become a stranger to myself and my life.
Trangott looked entirely unfamiliar, and James Feather, who had
not spoken to me since our conversation about the Lock
Hospital, seemed a creature from another world. Some part of
me heard them talking, but I seemed to float outside my body.

'What is the matter, Maria? You look a little feverish,'
Trangott said, uncharacteristically concerned. 'Go off to bed. I
will clear up here.'

It was not until the following week that I saw Rebecca
again, when the Women's Union met with a Member of
Parliament at Melrose House in Kalk Bay.

We had, at our annual meeting, unanimously passed a
motion to call for a debate in Parliament on extending the
vote to women. Those of us in the Franchise Committee went
to work immediately. One of the first steps was to persuade a
Member of Parliament to propose the debate in the Assembly.

Neville Melrose suggested that his parliamentarian friend,
Mr Orpen, might be open to the suggestion, and invited him
to lunch at the Coach House in Kalk Bay to meet us.
I explained to Trangott that there was a special meeting that

day, and I set off in the carriage sent by Rebecca.

We had no difficulty at all in persuading Mr Orpen. 'I have long wanted to propose such a debate,' he said, 'but it is not going to be easy. I suspect I am a lone voice. We need to have more members on our side when I raise this in the Assembly, so that we have a chance of winning the vote. A vote against might be more damaging to the cause than if we had not raised the issue at all.'

At one stage in the afternoon, Rebecca and I passed each other in the kitchen. We stopped, facing each other.

'Are you all right, Maria?' she asked.

'Not completely. It feels strange. As if the real me is somewhere else, far out at sea, with you.'

She smiled. 'Like gulls, flying low, just above the surface of the water.'

She put the tray she was carrying down on the table, took the multicoloured silk scarf from around her neck and softly, slowly put it around my shoulders. 'So that you can feel me all afternoon,' she said. And I did – the material caressing my neck and shoulders. And the memory of its scent, rosewater, fills me now with longing.

'A wife's work is to take care of her husband and children,' Trangott grumbled when I came home later that evening.

'No,' I said, observing his surprise, and not caring if it brought on a rage. 'No. My work is also to help those women who are in danger every day of their lives, and women who have no choice but to sell their bodies to men, often respectable men, like you, who have wives and children.'

'The police are there to protect them,' he bellowed.

'The police. The police! Do you know that in the last three months two more girls have been murdered and the police refuse to take these cases seriously? We at the Women's Union think it is the work of one man. The women at Dock Road Hotel call him the Strangler. There is also a rumour that the victims are raped – with a sharp instrument – after they are strangled. But the police ignore this – they will not even comment. It is obvious that they disregard these cases because the women are all prostitutes. Trangott,' I pleaded, 'women's lives are in danger!'

What I did not tell him, however, was that Rebecca was attempting to do something about it all. Many a night she would go to the Dock Road Hotel, and try to persuade the prostitutes there that they were in danger and to go with her instead to one of the Rescue Homes. I suspected, too, that she was also trying to identify the Strangler. I feared for her safety, and worried about the long carriage ride back to Kalk Bay late at night. Neville and I succeeded in persuading her to stay over some nights at Mrs Mackay's boarding house. This also had the advantage that she and I could meet at the Café Royal or the Company Gardens the next morning. And sometimes, we met in her room at Mrs Mackay's.

That period of my life was a maelstrom of alarm and joy, exhilaration and fear. I felt that I was picking my way over rocks at high tide. The rocks were slippery and sharp and often unsteady, and I felt I might at any minute plunge into the sea. At times it felt as if I had already fallen and was being battered against the rocks.

The worst aspect was the sense I had that I was neglecting my children. Although they all seemed to love Rebecca, I know that they sensed my preoccupation even when I was with them, helping with their schoolwork or caring for them when they were ill. The older ones – John and Bertha, particularly – seemed to notice my withdrawal, and in subtle and barely perceptible ways became especially demanding of my time and attention.

And Trangott, of course, had the strongest reaction. He seemed to know that he had lost some essential part of me, even though it was a part he had never really owned. His rages became more frequent, and this, in turn, further unsettled the children. Trangott did not know whether to blame my friendship with Rebecca or my involvement in the Women's Union – or, possibly, even my inability to have more children – for his loss of control over me.

I had to exercise great care whenever I slipped away to meet Rebecca. Despite the danger, we sent each other letters almost every day by Penny Post – the Post Coach could get a note from Kalk Bay to the centre of Cape Town in one or two days. I always tried to collect the post myself, and to hide Rebecca's letters far from Trangott's eyes, but I was not always successful and he would pull out an envelope addressed to me in Rebecca's distinctive, extravagant handwriting.

'What are these letters you are getting? Who writes to you so much?' He demanded one afternoon.

'They are the minutes of the Women's Union meetings that you refuse to allow me to attend,' I replied with spirit. 'We are busy with an important campaign, and I need to know what has been decided at the meetings.'

'You should be busy with important work here!' And he threw the envelope down on the table. 'You have not time to read letters all day. You have children to see to, and guests in the hotel.' He thrust his square face towards mine before turning on his heel. Alarmed at the intensity of his rage, I picked up the letter and put it in my bodice, keeping it there until I had an opportunity to read it at the Café Royal on my way to collect the laundry later in the day.

There, to the sweet sounds of the piano and the rich smell of coffee, I opened Rebecca's letter and let her words wash over me.

Maria

Today a gull perched on the balcony of my studio and looked at me with its round, solemn eyes. I told it about you – about your eyes and your mouth, about your serenity of soul that no drudgery can dull. I told it that your breasts are like the swell of a wave, that your skin smells of lemongrass, and tastes like seaspray. I told the gull about your nakedness, and how your calm waters become tidal waves at a touch. I told it about the cool peace of your rock pools, where exquisite colours glow in the moonlight ...

I kept Rebecca's letters in a locked box in the upstairs linen cupboard, unable to destroy them, as my common sense told me I should, and I read and re-read them whenever I had an opportunity.

All the while, I tried to avoid making Trangott suspicious. I thought I had managed this – until the day he had me followed. I was sitting in the Café Royal one morning, reading Rebecca's latest letter, half hoping she might arrive, when I noticed a woman at a table across the room, watching me. There was something familiar about her, but I could not remember where I had seen her before.

At first I thought I was imagining her eyes on me. Gradually, however, I became more suspicious. I had been there for about an hour, and the woman stayed all that time – long after she had finished her coffee. She was writing something in a notebook, and I saw her looking up at me every now and again.

Then, when I left, the woman followed me. That is when I was sure that Trangott had a hand in this. I tried to elude her among the people and the carriages as I hurried home. I slipped into the Germania and climbed the stairs. Trangott was not in his office, but I heard him soon enough at the foot of the stairs at the front door. I started to go down the stairs to investigate, and glimpsed him saying a hasty farewell to the woman who had followed me. After this, Rebecca and I were forced to meet somewhere else, away from curious eyes.

In the ward this morning, surrounded by disturbed women whose dull and desperate lives have probably never known any joy, I long for Rebecca's presence. And for a brief moment, I am transported back to when my body felt like a sea anemone closing over her.

circle seven

RE-MEMBERING

*Break a vase, and the love that reassembles the fragments
is stronger than that love which took its symmetry
for granted when it was whole.*

—Derek Walcott, *Nobel Prize acceptance speech, 1993*

Lesson Seven – Re-membering

Writing repairs the author
—Heléne Cixous, *Coming to Writing*

Autobiographical stories construct a self. In the process of writing our story, we collect those parts of ourselves that have been scattered. We re-member, we bring together, the fragments, which become whole again through the activity of the imagination.

Writing one's story is more than gathering information about oneself. In telling the stories of our life, we also change the stories of our life. The process alters us. It takes us back into the past, and changes our future.

In writing autobiography, the 'I' is both creator and creation – both writer and that which is written about. In this way, autobiography is self-discovery, self-invention, and self-re-presentation. By making ourselves 'present', we claim 'author-ity' over the experiences of the past.

Writing is the clenching of the fist against passivity. Women, in particular, often see themselves as passive bystanders in their own lives. Writing enables us to reclaim ourselves as protagonists in our life stories. Seeing ourselves as protagonists in our own lives allows us to re-invent ourselves. We become agents of our own story. By re-creating the self, writing also restores or repairs the self. It enables a shift in consciousness – an awakening.

- *Describe events in your life in which you felt as if you were a passive bystander in your own life. Try to identify a common feeling or emotion in them, and a pattern.*
- *Now create a scene in which you become an active protagonist in the experience described above – in which you break the pattern.*

Anna Bertrand,

Cape Town, 2004

I am seven years old, walking home from primary school through the suburb of Parkview, Johannesburg, with two school friends. A man appears from nowhere. 'Hullo, girls.' He is smiling, very friendly. 'I've got something to show you.' He's holding a small box in his hand.

We stop and look. He takes out a thing that looks like a thin brown balloon. 'Do you know what this is, what it's for?' We don't. I can't remember his explanation, but it was something about a Daddy being nice to a Mummy.

'Do you want me to show you how it works?' We are uncertain. He looks very friendly, and talks like an uncle who organises the games at children's birthday parties. But there is something else; a feeling, almost a smell of a feeling, that is underneath what is happening.

He starts to unzip his pants. All the time smiling, like a friendly uncle.

'Have you ever seen one of these?' He is holding something in his hand. The feeling gets worse, we know something is wrong. We want to run, but we are polite little girls and he is a grown-up. It is as if my feet are stuck to the ground. Heavy. I don't know how to get them to move. Then my one friend says, 'We must go, our mothers are waiting.' And we start to run. He calls after us.

I am eighteen, and have just missed the bus to university. A car stops at the bus stop and a man in a suit asks if I want a lift. He is about 40, quite plump. He looks the type that plays chess – very neat and clean, smelling of after-shave.

I get in, putting my satchel of books at my feet.

He turns off at Zoo Lake and into the road that winds around the lake. 'I always take this route, it's so relaxing,' he says. He stops the car under some trees and turns off the engine.

'Look at the ducks on the water ... so peaceful.'

That feeling again. Underneath the scent of his after-shave, the smell of that familiar feeling again. He casually puts an arm around my shoulder and his hand strokes my knee.

'You are very pretty. Just give me a nice kiss and then we'll go.'

A sour, stuck feeling. A numbness comes over me. I don't want to be here, but he is being so 'nice'. I try to think of something to say that won't offend him.

He takes my silence as agreement and fastens his open mouth on mine. His tongue thrusts in and his hand moves up my thigh.

I jerk and move away, move close to the door, trying to get his hands and mouth off me.

He seems not to notice my resistance. 'That was nice,' he says. 'Can I give you a lift again tomorrow? Same time?'

I nod, and he starts the car. He drives me to the University, asking friendly questions and telling me about his work.

I never wait at that bus stop at the same time, ever again.

⌣

I am 56. I have gone to examine the place where a woman was recently killed – the victim in a court-case I am monitoring. I want to see the spot where the accused is alleged to have thrown a sex-worker over the railings onto the rocks below. I park my car in the parking area of Queen's Beach and walk over to the railings. It is early evening, about five-thirty, but because it is winter, it is already nearly dark.

As I stand there, holding onto the railing and looking down onto the rocks and the rough sea below, I have an uneasy sense that someone is watching me. I look around but see nothing.

The sea is crashing against the rocks, and the north-wester tears at me.

I tell myself not to be stupid – that it is just a wild night, and there is the spirit of the murdered woman around – and decide to go down onto the beach. As I reach the bottom of the steps, I feel an elbow around my throat, while a hand pulls my arm behind my back.

'Keep walking,' a gruff instruction at my ear. I can feel his hot breath and smell the sourness – alcohol, cigarettes and something else that I don't recognise. A numbness comes over me and I walk as if mechanised, desperately trying to remember even one of the self-defence moves I learned at the women's anti-rape workshop.

He is choking me with his arm, and his body is pressed against my back. I try to struggle. A stifled shout for help.

'Shut up ... or I'll kill you!' He tightens his grip on my arm, and exerts more pressure on my throat.

I am now stumbling on the beach, the sand thick and soft. I try again to shout, 'Let me go!', hoping I sound confident and assertive. Don't show fear, I remember from the workshop. Rapists feel more powerful if you're passive.

But I am paralysed with fear. A familiar feeling of inertia, heaviness – only this time it is worse. A passivity that starts in my belly. Then, like an octopus, it reaches down my legs, along my arms, now heavy and lethargic. And then it spreads throughout my body, up into my throat, choking my voice, crawling into my cheekbones, behind my face, and into my brain, which becomes damp and spongy. Thoughts unable to connect.

He gives me a shove and I fall onto my hands and knees in the sand. Then he is on top of me, trying to push me onto my back, grabbing at his pants. Suddenly I seem to connect with myself, find my energy. This time I hear my angry shout. Furiously, I push him off. Kick out at him, my heel hitting him in the face. He comes at me again, lunging towards me. But I am ready this time, and kick as hard as I can. He shouts in pain and anger and rolls onto his side, doubled up, incongruously, in a foetal position.

I am up and running, totally intent on getting to my car before he can catch up with me. I run up the steps, two at a time. I glance over my shoulder. No sign of him, but it is too dark to see if he is still on the beach. I reach my car, my legs wobbly, my hands shaking as I fumble for the car keys in my pocket. Key in lock, turn, turn, open the door, inside, quickly lock the door, gear-lock stuck, tears of frustration, fear, find the ignition ...

There is a bang on the door, his face at the window, distorted, leering. A knife blade flashes.

The engine starts, jolts into gear, stalls, starts again. Just drive. Where are the lights? Drive through red robots, don't stop for anything. Home. Open my front door, lock it, check it is locked, check again, lean against the door, crying, shaking. Brandy, a hot bath, bed.

But no sleep. My cat knows something is wrong and stays awake with me. He sits bolt upright on the windowsill, keeping watch on the street below. At 2 am I give up trying to sleep and sit at the table with another brandy, wishing I still smoked.

Then, back in bed, I fall into a restless brandy-induced sleep, and wake in the morning groggy and shaky. I force myself to go for my morning walk on the beach. For the first time, I'm frightened to walk alone. But I can't let him change my life, I tell myself, so I put on my windbreaker and open the door. My fear seems to be lodged like a weight in my legs, but I keep walking.

———

Dear Maria

Yesterday, in the Archives, while doing some detective work on the Women's Christian Temperance Union and the campaigning you did around the vote for women, I found the transcript of the Debate in the House of Assembly of 25 July 1892.

A Mr Orpen moved that: *members consider a new clause to the Franchise and Ballot Bill to allow the vote to be extended to include female persons.*

Were you there, Maria, to hear John X Merriman's reply? *There is a distinction between the sexes which all the writing and gabble in the world will not bridge.* And were you upset when the members laughed and cheered as he continued: *I rather hold with the good old Dutch proverb that said women's counsel and brandy are two capital things but you must use them very cautiously.* And then finally, to more cheers: *God Almighty has made the sexes separate and no amount of legislation can possibly make it otherwise.*

It would surely have gratified you, though, when Mr Orpen, who seemed an enlightened man, said: *I pity those laughing, from the bottom of my heart. I am grieved to find that the House is not sufficiently up to the mark to vote for women's franchise.* He, at least, had vision, the foresight to believe that: *in a few years time female suffrage will be carried in the House in which we are sitting.*

But it took a lot longer than a few years. Sadly, within the next few years you yourself had died, and it took until 1930 – another 38 years – before the House of Assembly granted votes to women. And then it was to white women only.

Today in court, I was digging in my bag for my pen, so I didn't see Sebastian coming into the courtroom until I noticed a strange smell. That smell. The same smell as two nights ago when the man's arm was around my throat and his body pressed down on me on Queen's beach.

I stare in disbelief at Sebastian as he enters the witness box, nausea rising up in me. Could he have been my attacker? He stares back, mockingly. He has a moustache. I didn't notice a moustache on the distorted face of the man at my car window. But, I know from Nikki that Sebastian has been hanging around Sea Point.

I push down the nausea and try to focus on the trial. Sebastian is giving evidence in his own defence. I can't believe it, Maria. I can't believe the story he has come up with! He is claiming that Isobel was drunk and tried to kill herself by throwing herself over the railing. And that he, the hero, was trying to stop her. Between his and Mr Bellows's performances, you'd think he was a heartbroken lover.

'I still have nightmares about it', Sebastian says, and he actually wipes a tear from his cheek!

God. The Magistrate can't possibly fall for this one.

'Why did the witness say she saw you throw Miss Fransman over the railing?' Bellows asks him.

Sebastian smirks, 'She was too *gesuip*, too drunk to see anything.'

Who does he think he's fooling?

Now it is Nikki's turn. She squares her shoulders, tucks a stubborn lock of hair behind her ear, and goes for blood.

'So, you are saying you were trying to save Ms Fransman, not kill her?'

'*Ja.*' Sebastian nods at the Magistrate as if Nikki is not really there.

'Then, why wasn't it you who reported her fall to the police, why didn't you call Sea Rescue?'

'Because I could see she was dead?' he explains, 'and I was scared someone would say I did it.' He looks accusingly at Nikki.

'You could *see* she was dead. From up there? Nikki's face reflects the disdain in her voice. 'And the witness who said you were angry, who said that you threatened to kill Ms Fransman, was she making the story up?'

'*Ja.*' He nods again to Magistrate Van Deventer.

'Why would she do that?'

'To get me in trouble. She hates me.'

'Why is that, do you think?' Nikki's tone is suddenly disarmingly sweet.

'Don't know.' Sebastian manages to look victimised. '*Sy's net 'n hoer*, a prostitute like the other one.'

'So Ms Fransman was just a prostitute – so you felt that you had the right to kill her? To punish her, or just for fun? Is that what you think, Mr Sebastian?'

'I didn't kill her. I tried to stop her.'

'Why? If she was only a prostitute, why go to all that trouble?'

Sebastian mutters, 'Don't know.'

Nikki fixes her relentless eyes on his miserable face.

'Mr Sebastian, is that all you can come up with? That this woman was trying to kill herself and you tried to stop her? What possible reason could she have had for trying to commit suicide, and why at that moment?'

Sebastian is beginning to lose his smugness.

'How should I know! *Sy was net 'n hoer.*'

'Yes', Nikki pounces, 'and we know what you think of prostitutes, don't we? They don't matter, do they? They are just rubbish to be thrown away. Aren't they, Mr Sebastian?'

'Ja.' Nikki is starting to get to Sebastian. He wipes his neck, and his voice is shaky.

'But it is not just prostitutes, is it, Mr Sebastian? It is women you hate, isn't it? They should all be got rid of. Isn't that what you think, Mr Sebastian?'

'Ja – hulle's almal hoere!' Sebastian spits out the words at Nikki. *'Jy ook! Julle's almal vuilgoed,* all rubbish!'

He glares around, contemptuously.

'Yes, that is what the witness, Judith, tells us she heard you say as you threw Ms Fransman onto the rocks. She says you shouted, *"Vuilgoed"*.'

Nikki leaves it there, satisfied that she has made her point.

Magistrate Van Deventer adjourns for the day, saying he will give judgment and pass sentence tomorrow.

'You were great, Nikki,' I tell her later. 'The Magistrate should find him guilty and put him away for life!'

'Well, let's not get too excited. I'm never certain with Magistrate Van Deventer.'

Her eyes smile at me behind her glasses.

I tell her about the attack on me in Sea Point, and that I think it might have been Sebastian. 'But I can't be sure. Maybe all rapists smell the same.'

'I'm so sorry. You must have been terrified. How are you feeling now?' Her eyes rest gently on me.

'OK – thanks. I still feel shaky, but it was useful in a strange way,' I say. 'It felt like some kind of a turning point. I've been in a stuck place for a long time, and it made me fight back. I'm just glad to be alive.'

Nikki smiles again, 'I'm glad, too.'

She seems genuinely concerned about me and really pleased I'm OK. I start to wonder about her. She has never mentioned a husband or children. But – she certainly isn't my type. She's too warm, too sane, too cheerful. Not that my type is good for me, though. Maybe I should consider changing my type, Maria, now that I've had a wake-up call.

As I leave, I check that Sebastian is nowhere in sight. I am still jittery from the attack. Was it so dangerous and unsafe for women in your day, Maria? Could you or Rebecca go down to Queen's Beach at night, without fear of rapists and murderers?

Perhaps that is what happened to Rebecca. Is that how she died? Had she been to a Women's Union meeting in Sea Point? And had you hoped to slip out after dinner to catch the end of the meeting and see her? And did Trangott go out himself, leaving you to see to the after-dinner coffee, whisky and cigars in the lounge?

Did Rebecca wait a while for you, and then decide to go down to Queens Beach? She was restless, perhaps she wanted to walk in the night air and be alone. She stood holding onto the railing, staring down at the waves crashing onto the rocks. It was high tide, and the turbulence of the waves matched her swirling mood. She was thinking of you, wanting to be with you, to touch you, wrap her long-limbed body around you and breathe in your scent.

Then, perhaps, she walked down the steps onto the beach. In the darkness she felt an arm around her throat. She struggled and kicked out wildly, wrenching herself out of his grip. She turned to face her assailant and gasped as she called out his name. He put both his hands around her throat and squeezed until the night fell silent once more.

He let her body fall onto the soft sand, stared down at her for a moment, and then disappeared into the darkness.

Tonight I hear again the sweet melodies the pianist used to play at the Café Royal. And the sound of the sea – a roar as if the tide is coming in. A memory breaks through – like the cry of a gull, defiant against the dark. A memory of the morning my voice died, the morning Neville came to the hotel to tell me that Rebecca's body had been found on Queen's Beach.

I stared at him, unable to comprehend him, or comfort him. There was nothing to say, nothing that could be said. And from that moment, I never uttered a word again.

The police questioned the women at the Women's Union meeting. They said that when they had left, Rebecca was standing at the door of the hall, looking as if she were waiting for someone. I didn't tell them it was me she was waiting for. The police also questioned Neville. Initially they were suspicious, not understanding how a man would let his sister walk around Sea Point on her own at night.

They also questioned Trangott when they heard that he had been out that night and could not account for his whereabouts. But they couldn't come up with a motive for Trangott and released him. Little did they know that the reason he went out that night was to try to calm down after finding out about me and Rebecca.

That afternoon, when I got back to the hotel after collecting the laundry, Trangott had been waiting for me. He called me into the office. His face was red and perspiring. He was spluttering and struggling with his English. He gestured to an opened envelope on the desk and a letter beside it. I recognised Rebecca's handwriting immediately.

'This letter. It is from that Rebecca Melrose? It is written to you?' He was breathing heavily and his neck seemed to swell up.

'Yes,' I replied, feeling a strange calm coming over me. 'Yes, it is.'

'To you? To you? She writes these things? To you? About breasts? About kissing and who knows what else! To you! My wife! *My* wife!'

I can't remember what I started to say, but he would not let me continue.

'We talk about it later. I am too upset now. I must get out of here.' He said this through a tight mouth, his fists clenching and unclenching, probably in an attempt not to hit me.

I heard him stamp down the stairs and then the front door slam shut. I picked up Rebecca's letter with trembling fingers, and put it in my apron pocket.

There was a Women's Union meeting that evening in Sea Point, but I thought better of going. Better to wait for him and talk to him. But he didn't come back at dinner time. I served the guests, cleaned up the kitchen, helped Georgina with her schoolwork, and eventually went to bed.

It was after two in the morning when Trangott returned. I

heard him banging things in the kitchen, and braced myself for his entrance into our bedroom. I had rehearsed what I was going to say to him. But I heard him go through to the lounge instead.

The next morning I found him asleep on the couch. I left him there, got the children up, and went to the kitchen to prepare breakfast. Which is where Neville found me.

Why had I not stopped Trangott from going out that night? Why hadn't I insisted on talking to him? And, why hadn't I risked his anger and gone to meet Rebecca after the meeting? If I had, Rebecca might be alive today, and I would not be lying here, in this place, listening to the sounds of a ghostly piano and distant crashing waves.

Anna Bertrand,

Cape Town, 2004

Dear Maria

Died yesterday.

Not you, Maria, but Dorothy Feather. In her Valkenberg case record dated 22 January 1944, it states: *Died yesterday at 1.30pm.* She was 85. In the previous observation recorded the year before, on 10 October 1943, the record states: *Helpless, and general condition has been deteriorating. Confined to bed in clinic. Quite demented.* The records in Dorothy's file state that she had had *no visitors since admission.*

I find a copy of her death notice in the file. It reads:

NOTICE OF DEATH
Mental Disorders Act 1916
(General Regulations 38, 40, 69)
21 January 1944

I hereby give you notice that DOROTHY MARY FEATHER of the District of Cape Town, a paying patient, Registered No. F99, received into this Institution on the 29th day of October 1891, died therein on the 21st day of January 1944 at the age of 85 years, after an illness of prolonged duration; and I further certify that Dr E Cloete attended the said Dorothy Mary Feather during the illness which terminated in death, and that the apparent cause of death of the said patient was *senility.*

Final diagnosis of mental condition *dementia praecox.*

Here, too, in the file, is a letter dated 6 March 1944, two months after Dorothy's death, from the Valkenberg Superintendent to the Secretary of the Colonial Orphan Chamber and Trust Company (which administered the Trust money from James Feather's will). It reads:

Sir
The undermentioned is a list of possessions belonging to the late DOROTHY MARY FEATHER, and I shall be glad if you would notify me as soon as possible the method of their disposal.

Vests – 6
Bloomers – 2
Petticoats – 3

Yours faithfully
Physician Superintendent

Another death: Trangott died a few days after Rebecca. Were their deaths connected? It doesn't say on his Death Notice what he died of – only that he was 58 years old. That's still relatively young. Was it a heart attack? I imagine him a big man, prone to bursts of temper, and perhaps, because he preferred to eat heavy German food, his heart gave in. But why just then?

And here, in the Annual Report on Asylums, which dates back to 1889, the reasons are given for people being committed. Most of the Valkenberg inmates were admitted under Section 27 – for 'ordinary lunatics'. But you were admitted under Section 36. I looked up the regulations to find out what Section 36 meant: *Section 36 applies when a Magistrate or Court has ordered a person's removal to an Asylum.*

Can that be right, Maria – were you admitted by a Magistrate? Did you go to court, and were you sentenced to Valkenberg? Why? What for? What did you do? Was it perhaps because they thought you had killed Trangott? Did you, Maria? Did you kill him? Because he was the one who had strangled Rebecca?

Did he find out about your relationship, work himself into a rage, and then find and kill her? Maybe he had intended only to confront her – but was overcome with fury, and ended up strangling her.

Did he perhaps tell you he had done this? After they questioned and released him, did he gloat at your grief, did he shout that now you could go back to being a proper wife? Did he shake you to make you speak, to make you cry? Did he demand sex with you to reclaim his right to your body?

And did you pick up the carving knife from the sideboard and sink it into his throat as he came towards you? Did you?

The memories of that time are like scattered fragments.

How long had I had been standing there, over Trangott's sprawled body, holding the knife and watching the blood spurt from his throat, when John found me? I remember him trying to take the knife out of my hand, but my fingers had closed around it and I could not move. Then the stiffness moved down my arm and through my whole body, and I fell down.

When I woke later in the hospital bed, I was paralysed.

The police arrested me for Trangott's murder. A few weeks later, I was put on trial. The police and then the Magistrate tried to extract a confession from me, or at least to get me to nod my head in response to their questions. But how could I, when I did not remember any details at all about that terrible night?

I do remember how cold it was that day in court.

They brought me in from the hospital, wheeled me into the court room, and placed me behind the wooden stand. As I passed the benches, I saw my children sitting in the front row, all except Georgina. Where was she, I wondered, who was looking after her, how was she coping with the terrible thing that had broken her life apart?

I stared around me, while the prosecutor encouraged me to answer – either with words or a nod. My cousins from Constitution Street were sitting behind my family, and Sophia with them. And I recognised my neighbours – Miss Dryer and Arthur Boyes, as well as Mrs Mackay from the boarding house. In fact, it seemed that nearly everyone who lived in Church and Long Streets was there.

Neville Melrose was there, looking ill. I remember him coming to see me in hospital a few days before. I think he wanted to believe I had killed Trangott, hoping that the person who killed Rebecca had been punished.

And there, like a rat with its whiskers bristling, was James Feather. Why was he there? As I looked at him, there was something I seemed to remember about him – a certain smell perhaps. But my mind was sluggish and my memory was like a dammed-up river.

As I watched the waning afternoon sun through the windows behind the Magistrate, I found it hard to keep my mind on what was going on around me. Perhaps that is what the Magistrate meant by demented when he declared me unfit to stand trial. A lunatic. To be admitted to an asylum.

I felt nothing except a resigned numbness when I was moved here, my fate decided. I have sat here each day since, as I do now, gazing out of the day room window at the trees beyond, listening to the sound of wind and birds, and hearing, at times, the plaintive notes of a piano and the sound of waves far away.

Slowly, out of the empty deadness, I am beginning to put the pieces together, gather up the fragments.

Perhaps now, I too am at last ready to die.

circle eight

LETTING GO

When I ask a gift from my death,
it is that at the last minute I will be able
to look back over my life and know without doubt,
the entire story I have been living.

—Deena Metzger, *Writing for Your Life*

Dear Maria

On this grey, drizzly morning, I have come here to Kalk Bay, to the church graveyard where Rebecca is buried, to sit and write to you for the last time. I imagine, speculate, wonder again, about the events in that turbulent time of your life. You probably didn't get to Rebecca's funeral. A few days after Rebecca's death, Trangott himself was dead, and you were on trial for his murder. You were not able to mourn her at her grave, and that's why I've come here today, to say goodbye to Rebecca for you, hoping it will help me, too, to let go – of you.

Last night, I sat up late. I wrote for hours, by candlelight, at my table, while listening over and over to a recording of Bruch's cello piece, *Kol Nidrei*. I was determined to cross unknown thresholds in myself. I wanted my writing to break through, to burst onto the page, so that I could find an ending, a resolution. The candlelight and plaintive, rich notes, helped me in my search. I wrote into the darkness, into the unknown and unknowing, the place of no defences, writing to touch the tender, bruised places in myself. I wrote towards the place my workbook calls 'a risky country situated somewhere near the unconscious'. It says 'you have to go through the back door of thought' to find the unconscious, your buried self.

The south-easter was still last night. As I wrote, in the empty time between night and day, the world seemed to hold its breath. A distant dog barked and then fell silent, and the time and place that separates us – the skin between you and me – seemed to dissolve. I heard your voice and saw your words appearing on the page before me. I felt your breath in the rise and fall of my own breast.

I have felt you, these past weeks, as a constant presence in my life. Perhaps, too, that particular winter so many years ago, I was in the margins of your dying life, waiting to gather the fragments as you let them fall. That last night, in Valkenberg, during a moment that seemed to be a crack in the night, it may be that I drew your last breath with you, and have held it, suspended, until now.

Writing is Learning to Die

I lie on the inside of the night
at the edge of the wound
scratching the dark with my eyelids
ready to write the story
which I cannot bear to remember

What is it that makes one dare?

I write as if the secret that is in me
were before me
galloping ahead of me and beyond –
a night-ride to the very edge of the world
where all the dragons live

What is it that makes one dare?

I let go into a moment of nothing
allow a force that I am not
recount my story to me
allow its breath to enter me
inspire me – and

I hear writing write

A woman was already here, when I arrived this morning. I unlatched the wooden gate leading into the garden and saw her sitting on the bench overlooking Rebecca's grave. Her head was bowed.

I did not want to disturb her – perhaps, like me, she had come here to be alone – so I walked around the edge of the garden and came to sit here on a stone bench, under a tree at the other end of the graveyard. It was raining softly.

I wish I had been able to find your grave, Maria, to have a sense of the place where your body lies buried and to see a gravestone with your name on it. Instead, my notebook is balanced on my knee as I sit on this bench, looking towards Rebecca's grave.

I want to tell you about yesterday, in court, when Magistrate Van Deventer gave his judgment in Sebastian's case. As the Magistrate swept into court, his black gown flowing behind him, we all stood and waited for him to settle himself before taking our seats again. It's all so theatrical, this courtroom stuff, I thought – with its ceremony and ritual.

Sebastian seemed anxious for the first time. Even Mr Bellows looked paler and less bulky. I glanced across at Nikki. She also seemed a little strained, as if she had not slept well.

'Mr Sebastian.' Magistrate Van Deventer put his finger to his spectacles and pushed them up onto the bridge of his nose.

'I have considered all the evidence in this case ...' He paused, seeming to look into his eyebrows for the answer.

'... and find you...' Again a pause. We all held our breath.

'... guilty – of the murder of Pauline Fransman, on the 17th of June 2004.'

I let out my breath, and again looked across at Nikki. I saw her shoulders relax.

'In considering an appropriate sentence, I have taken into account the fact that the State has a duty to send a message to the community that it does not take violence against women lightly.' He coughed, adjusting his spectacles again.

'The fact that the deceased was a prostitute can have no bearing on my judgment, nor the sentencing. A woman was murdered, and I must impose a sentence that reflects the seriousness of the crime.'

He paused again, as if to let his words sink in. Who was he kidding, Maria, why mention the fact that she was a prostitute if it has 'no bearing'?

'I therefore sentence you to fifteen years imprisonment.'

The minimum sentence. If he really wanted to show how seriously he took crimes against women, he would have sent Sebastian to jail for longer. I looked across at Nikki again. She nodded to me. I smiled back, consoling myself with the thought that fifteen years is fifteen years, and Sebastian will not be able to hurt any other women in that time.

Sebastian didn't react at first, just stared at the Magistrate, then turned to look around, his bloodshot eyes defiant. He managed a grin as they led him away, but his body had lost its jauntiness and hung as if defeated.

I had a strange sense, as they took him away, that something more than just this case was over, that something bigger and older had finally been settled.

I see you, Maria and Dorothy, in the day room after lunch. Most of the women are dozing in their chairs, their heads slumped onto their chests, when Dorothy pulls her chair up to yours and grasps your hand.

'... water ... she's gone ... too much water .... rocks ... blood on the rocks ...'

She whimpers and repeats, 'blood on the rocks ...'

What rocks, Dorothy? Whose blood? Tell me, Dorothy, tell me.

She lets go of your hand and begins wringing at her overall, her knuckles white with effort.

'... no one must see ... the rocks ... push her over ... push ... push ...'

Who? Dorothy? Who was pushed? Who mustn't see?

'... blue dress ... all torn ... Hester, mustn't cry ... too much water ...'

Maria, would that I could help Dorothy still her restless hands, help her unravel her jumbled words, help her tell her story. But it is your voice that resonates in me, it is your ending I must write, your scattered fragments I must gather up, and with you, re-member your story – and find its ending.

Later that night, the ward locked up for the night, you and Dorothy are surrounded by the shapes of the other women in their beds, restless in the moonlight. You lie awake as usual, listening to Dorothy, '... too much water ... rocks ... died ... want to die ...'

How do you want it to end, Maria? What fragments do you need to re-member, to complete the circle, so that you can let go? The fragment that tells of Trangott's death? Was it really you who killed him? Is this the inevitable end to your story? It seems, indeed, to be the only action that makes sense of the story. It made sense to others at the time – the police, John and the other children, and probably the people in court that day. It would most likely have made sense to Mrs Mackay, who was sitting behind John and Bertha in court. She had known you for many years, and knew how often you visited Rebecca when she stayed overnight at her boarding house. She may even have been aware of the nature of your relationship. If she thought Trangott had killed Rebecca, she might have thought it made sense for you to avenge her death. Neville, too, would want the story to end in this way.

But there is another picture, hazy at first, that comes like a wisp of mist over the window ledge of the ward as you lie there in the moonlight, listening to Dorothy's urgent ramblings, and you try to remember.

The picture gradually becomes clearer, and, through your eyes, I see Trangott sitting exhausted at the writing desk next to the sideboard after being questioned that day by the police. I see a figure appear at the sideboard, argue with Trangott, threaten him. Then I see the figure pick up a knife from the sideboard and I see his arm come down, plunging the knife into Trangott's throat.

The man's back is towards you, so he doesn't see you standing at the kitchen door. He doesn't look round, but swiftly makes for the door. You hear his footsteps as he moves hurriedly down the stairs and out the front door into Church Street. He doesn't see you, but you see him. And you know, at that moment, whose hands were around Rebecca's neck, and who stopped her breath – and your life with it.

Things moved quickly after that. You went over to Trangott, took the knife from his throat, and there John found you, staring down at the limp, square body of his father, his blood splattered on the papers on the writing desk. They came and arrested you, they sentenced you, and packed you away into the asylum, dusty and forgotten.

But the petals are beginning to fall, Maria. One by one, they fall to the ground. And here is the faintest perfume of roses – the touch of Rebecca's breath on your cheek.

The woman sitting at Rebecca's grave lifts her head. For a moment, she looks like the woman I'd noticed, then followed, that day at the Café Mozart – the woman who reminded me of you, Maria. She stands up now and carefully places something on Rebecca's gravestone. What is it? A flower? A letter? Then she turns and walks away, goes out the wooden gate and disappears, out of sight, down the road.

I wait a while, and then go over to Rebecca's grave. I can't find what the woman put there. I place the stone and the rose I brought on your behalf, then I stand awhile, my head bowed.

I feel my heart break at the thought of letting you go, Maria. I have loved you, and wept for you, all of my life.

In discovering your story, I have restored parts of myself that have been scattered, hidden, and forbidden. But to reclaim my own story, I know I must let you go. We are near the end of our telling, Maria. The fragments of our stories merge – your story has become mine, my truth yours.

I feel your dying, Maria, and let go of your last breath. I am left with a sweet sadness, like a melody played slowly, softly.

'You booked a table for three? Who else is joining us?' Nikki Cody looks like an untidy duck, her bright eyes inquiring and humorous behind her large blue-framed specs.

'No one.' Anna glances at the third place set at the table. 'Except the ghost of my great-grandmother. She died here, you know, in Valkenberg, over a hundred years ago.'

Looking around, Nikki notices the contorted shape of a tree outside the window. It is this tree that gives the restaurant its name – The Wild Fig.

'This used to be the Manor House, the residence of the former Superintendent, Dr Dodds. He was here in my great-grandmother's time. The restaurant owner has tried to preserve the old building.'

'What was her name, your great-grandmother? Why was she here?'

'Maria. Maria Jacoba Bertrand Schultz. They thought she'd murdered her husband, my great-grandfather, Trangott.'

'Did she?'

'I don't think so. I think it was someone else, a man called James Feather. He'd also raped his two daughters and then locked them away in asylums so they couldn't tell anyone.'

'What? That he raped them?'

'Yes, and that he'd murdered a young woman, Emily Booth. My theory is that his daughter, Dorothy, knew about Emily's murder and tried to tell people – so he had her certified insane.'

'Oh. But then why did they think it was your great-grandmother who'd murdered Trangott.'

'A revenge killing – they thought Trangott had killed Rebecca Melrose, the woman my great-grandmother was in love with.'

'Did he?'

'No, I don't think so. I think James Feather killed Rebecca too, when he found her walking one evening on Queen's Beach. I believe he was the 'Strangler' – the man who used to kill women, mainly sex-workers. And I suspect Trangott had gone there the same evening – quite by coincidence – to confront Rebecca about her relationship with Maria. Trangott witnessed the murder, and that's why James Feather had to kill him.'

'Did this James Feather ever get caught? Go to jail?'

'No – not for any of it – not for the rape of his daughters, nor for the other murders which he'd probably committed. He hated women, you see. But – and this might sound strange – I think that today, in court, you helped put him away.

'Glad to be of service.' Nikki smiled, 'So it runs in your family, does it?'

'What, murder?'

'No. Loving women.'

Anna felt herself flush. 'Yes, I suppose it does.'

'Tell me her story, then, this Maria of yours.'

Author's note

For those readers who like to separate 'facts' from 'fiction', the following might be of interest:

- Dorothy Feather was a real person, and her records are quoted verbatim from the sources acknowledged below.
- Various people in the book – including Dr Dodds, Superintendent of Valkenberg Asylum, Mr John X Merriman, MP, and Mr Orpen MP, were all actual historical figures, and quotes attributed to them are authentic.
- Other characters in the book are entirely creations of my imagination.
- The court case that Anna monitors is based on a real case: the murder of 27-year old Elizabeth Frazenburg, a sex-worker known as 'Isobel', who was killed by being flung over the railings at Queen's beach, Sea Point, on 21 November 1999. However, unlike the fictionalised version in this book, the case has not had a speedy resolution. Although the accused in the case, Mr Sebastian Fillis, was arrested the same day, the case has been postponed 26 times in the past five years – mostly due to the non-appearance of Mr Fillis, who was out on R10 000 bail. In December 2004, the case was postponed to 27 and 28 June 2005, for further trial.
- Extracts have been quoted, verbatim, from the following sources:
  Admission certificate (Circle Three):
  Valkenberg Hospital Collection, Valkenberg Hospital
      – Lunacy Register 1891 – 1915
      – Case book – Female admissions
  Entries from patient records (Circles Three, Six and Seven):
  Valkenberg Hospital Collection, Valkenberg Hospital
      – Patient records 1891 – 1920
  Will (Circle Three), letters from the Colonial Orphan Chamber and Trust Company (Circle Six and Seven) and Death Notice (Circle Seven):
  Valkenberg Hospital Collection, Valkenberg Hospital
      – Patient records 1891 – 1920
- Quotes from newsletters and minutes of meetings of the Women's Christian Temperance Union (Circles Five and Six):
  The White Ribbon, newsletter of the Women's Christian Temperance Union. 1890 – 1915
  Stapleton, FA, *Brief history of the Women's Christian Temperance Union in SA* (CT 1939)

Tiltman, Amanda. *The Women's Christian Temperance Union of the Cape Colony: 1889 – 1910*

- Record of the debate on the women's vote (Circle Seven), and statement by the Attorney-General, TL Graham (Circle Five):
  Cape of Good Hope: Debates in the House of Assembly:
  3 June – 29 August 1892
  Hansard – Cape House of Assembly debates: 1892
- *Cape Times* article, 20 March, 1889
- Ideas, inspiration, and quotations at the beginning of Circles and Lessons, as well as lines in the 'found poem' on page 194 are taken from the following sources:

  Cixous, H. *Coming to Writing and Other Essays.* Ed. Deborah Jenson. 1991 (Harvard University Press, Cambridge, Mass.)

  Cixous, H. *Rootprints: Memory and Life Writing.* 1997 (Routledge, London)

  Cixous, H. *Three Steps on the Ladder of Writing.* 1993 (Columbia University Press, New York)

  Elbow, P, *Writing with Power.* 1981 (Oxford University Press, New York)

  Griffin, S, *A Chorus of Stones.* 1992 (The Women's Press, London)

  Heilbrun, C. *Writing a Woman's Life.* 1989 (The Women's Press, London)

  Keating, A. *Women Reading Women Writing.* 1996 (Temple University Press, Philadelphia)

  Deena Metzger. *Writing for Your Life.* 1992 (Harper, San Francisco)

  Rainer, T. *Your Life as Story.* 1998 (Putnam, New York)

  Woolf, Virginia. *Moments of Being: Autobiographic Writings.* Ed. Jeanne Schulkind. 2002 (Pimlico, London)
- Other References and Resource Material
  Cape Almanac 1883, 1884, 1885
  Valkenburg Hospital, Superintendent's Office,
    – Register of patients, Feb 1891 – Dec 1915
    – Report on patients, Feb 1891 – Mar 1917
  Report of the Inspector of Asylums for the year ending 31st December 1896

(Note: patient's names have been changed in accordance with Valkenberg Hospital regulations).

Anne Schuster lives in Cape Town where she teaches creative writing.